GERRY ANDERSON'S

CAPTAIN SCARLET™

AND THE

MYSTERONS

SPV, Angel Interceptor, Cloudbase and associated Spectrum and World Security vehicles

First published in October 2017

A catalogue record for this book is available from the British Library

ISBN 978 1 78521 143 0

Library of Congress catalog card no. 2017933523

Published by Haynes Publishing, Sparkford, Yeovil, Somerset BA22 7JJ, UK
Tel: 01963 440635
Int. tel: +44 1963 440635
Website: www.haynes.com

Haynes North America, Inc.,
859 Lawrence Drive, Newbury Park, California 91320, USA

Printed in Malaysia.

Author Sam Denham
Illustrator Graham Bleathman
Editor Steve Rendle
Design James Robertson

All illustrations by Graham Bleathman with additional art by Chris Thompson
(pages 28, 61, 88, 93, 98), Richard Farrell (pages 38 and 39) and Mike Trim
(pages 68 and 72). Frontispiece illustration on page 7 by Mark Thomas.

Author's Acknowledgements
Thanks to Anderson Entertainment, Barry Davies, Theo de Klerk, Alan Shubrook,
David Thornhill, Nick Williams and Mike Jones of Fanderson.

Illustrator's Acknowledgements
Des Shaw, Hilton Fitzsimmons, Lee Elliott, Stephen Brown, Graeme Bassett,
Dolby and Pixel for art supervision and Katie Bleathman for tea, sympathy and
cat wrangling!

Spectrum gratefully acknowledges the assistance of Fanderson, the official
Gerry Anderson appreciation society for their help in the production of this
Manual. Visit www.fanderson.org.uk.

GERRY ANDERSON'S
CAPTAIN SCARLET
AND THE
MYSTERONS

SPV, Angel Interceptor, Cloudbase and associated Spectrum and World Security vehicles

Spectrum Agents' Manual

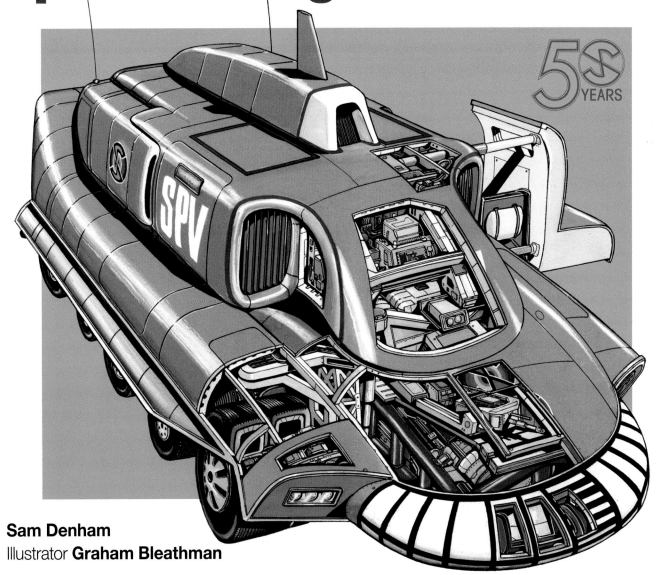

Sam Denham
Illustrator **Graham Bleathman**

Author's note

In 1966 the creators of Thunderbirds, the futuristic puppet series based on the daring exploits of International Rescue, were at the height of their success. Led by producers Gerry and Sylvia Anderson, the inventive team responsible for developing the world's most advanced puppet making technique – known as Supermarionation – had seen their latest series become another world-wide hit. Like earlier Supermarionation shows *Supercar*, *Fireball XL5* and *Stingray*, *Thunderbirds* presented a technologically advanced vision of the future where space-age heroes and heroines were launched into high-powered adventures aboard dynamic super-machines.

With each new series, characters and storylines became more sophisticated, and the action more realistic and believable, while the popularity of the Andersons' programmes resulted in spin-offs that included toys, games and other merchandise, and the creation of a multi-media empire that encompassed books, records, comic strips and feature films. The increasingly convincing worlds in which the Supermarionation series were set also led to the creation of a fictional universe which combined elements of the TV programmes in a vision of tomorrow that was first fully realised with the launch of the pioneering boys' comic *TV21* in 1965.

Presenting the Andersons' caricatured puppet originals in a visually naturalistic manner, the *TV21* comic strips helped accelerate the quest for realism in the filmed adventures. This was demonstrated in the first Supermarionation feature film *Thunderbirds Are Go*, which took the studio's small-scale tomorrow's world to new degrees of believability and paved the way for a revolutionary approach to film puppetry. Replacing the company's traditional large- headed marionettes, perfectly proportioned puppets were created for the Andersons' latest TV series, the first to be made under their company's new name, which had been changed in 1966 from AP Films to the forward-looking Century 21 Productions. Drawing on the more realistic style of the *TV21* comic and developing the darker elements of earlier TV shows, the established formula of cool-headed heroes taking on cold-hearted villains took on a chilling new form in the first series produced using the new hyper-realistic form of Supermarionation.

In a united world living in peace, and enjoying the benefits of modern technology, a new mysterious foe threatens everyday existence. Establishing an on-screen link with the *Thunderbirds Are Go* feature film, the new threat would result from the discovery of a strange alien city by a Zero X Martian expedition.

Destroying the city in a moment of panic, the spaceship's crew unleashes a force that threatens retaliation against the planet Earth using the mysterious power of retro-metabolism – the ability to recreate matter that has previously been destroyed. Earth's only hope is a newly formed security organisation – Spectrum – and its leading agent, once a victim of the alien's influence, but now a virtually indestructible hero.

Launched in 1967 with the support of a co-ordinated promotional campaign in *TV21*, *Captain Scarlet and the Mysterons* once again showcased the artistic inventiveness and technical ability of the Supermarionation team. Reaching new heights of cinematic perfection, the series became one of the Andersons' most memorable creations, presenting a vision of the 21st century where the wonders of modern science and technology face a malevolent otherworldly menace.

Welcome to the world of Captain Scarlet and the Mysterons.

CONTENTS

INTRODUCTION

MEMBERS OF SPECTRUM

From the moment official approval for the formation of our organisation was initially granted by the World Government, Spectrum has grown from the seed of an idea to become a fully functioning operational reality. Charged with the responsibility of providing highly progressive global security, and answerable only to the World President, within a few short years it has become the most efficient and technically advanced organisation of its kind, entirely prepared to take on the role for which it was created. In their steadfast determination to realise this challenging vision, I must commend all Spectrum personnel for the tireless dedication they have shown.

But when the proposal to form our organisation was first approved by the World Senate in 2065, it could never have been predicted that Spectrum would very soon serve a purpose for which its creation was never originally intended. As we all know, since that fateful day earlier this year when the mission to Mars led by Captain Black resulted in unforeseen disaster, Spectrum has taken on a new and vitally important role.

Our world is now threatened by a mysterious alien power, known only as the Mysterons, which has vowed to exact revenge for an inexplicably unprovoked attack on its Martian complex. All Spectrum's resources and personnel are now committed to combating this unearthly and unpredictable menace, and given the urgent nature of this challenge, it was felt essential to produce this manual as a means to aid all Spectrum operatives in effectively fulfilling this task.

In the manual's pages can be found profiles of all Spectrum's leading agents and specifications of the advanced vehicles and equipment designed for their use, in addition to the latest data about other organisations, installations and craft that may provide invaluable support in Spectrum's operational effectiveness. Operatives are also provided with the most up to date verifiable facts about the Mysteron menace, essential information about the latest weapons that are being developed against this intangible foe, and highly confidential details of Spectrum's most vital asset in its continuing battle to defend our planet. This information is further supplemented by reports on all Mysteron activity recorded to date in the continuing war of nerves being waged against our world.

It only remains for me to express my sincere gratitude for the vital contributions you are all making to ensure the security of the Earth, and the hope that our efforts will ultimately prove successful.

Spectrum is Green

White.

Colonel White
Commander-in-Chief

THIS IS 2068

Over the course of the last quarter century the majority of the world's inhabitants have enjoyed peace and prosperity under the guidance and control of the World Government, following the historic first official meeting of the World Senate on 23 June 2043. This new era in world unification was formally inaugurated three years later on 14 June 2046 when leading senators from member nations signed the Treaty of Tranquility under the World Government's loyal flag. Banning acts of war and aggression between countries, and binding them together to fight for one cause - the defence of the Earth - the treaty was left unsigned by only a handful of countries, including Translapvia and Slovburgh, Kwang Xavier, Tong Vietkin, Kulanki, Ching Quoy, Bereznik and the Republic of Britain, although the latter subsequently became a member

before the end of the decade following the overthrow of its military dictatorship in 2047.

Normally based at Unity City, the purpose-built metropolis constructed above the reefs of Bermuda, the World Government is led by a democratically elected president - the latest incumbent being James Younger, who replaced the long-serving Nikita Bandranaik at the end of his last term of office in 2066. Due to recent modernisation and reconstruction work being carried out at Unity City however, Younger's first term of office has coincided with a temporary move by the World Senate to the experimental North American sky tower complex Futura City, which has been accorded world capital status for the duration of the relocation. It is from here that all decisions regarding the administration of the planet are currently being made by senators representing

all the major countries and continents of the world. These include President Roberts, the current president of the United American States, the Triumvirate of Europe - John L. Henderson, Joseph Meccini and Conrad Olafson - and the deputy director of the United Asian Republic assembly, where elections for a new director are currently underway.

Primary concerns of the World Government are to ensure the provision of food supplies and power to the world's population. New and more efficient means of managing agriculture and food production are continually being sought in addition to the development of traditional methods. Irrigation of previously barren land is a priority, with arid inland areas now being made fertile through the use of immense desalinisation plants such as those at Nahama in the foothills of the Andes which processes sea water from the Pacific to increase crop yields in the land mass of South America. Similar techniques to irrigate desert areas in North America have been introduced by the World Food Organisation in North Africa, where a chain of subterranean lakes beneath the Sahara have been tapped at a control centre in Kufra to provide water for what is now one of the largest corn production sectors of the planet.

In addition to supplying drinking water to large urban populations, reservoirs and dams such as those at Boulder in

California and the currently under construction Manicougan dam in Canada have also been designed to provide a source of energy through tried and tested hydro-electric schemes, while the Earth's resources are concurrently being exploited to create a new energy source for the world's inhabitants using the revolutionary process of thermic power. Releasing energy from beneath the earth through the system's Nevada mother station, this raw power is converted into thermal waves and beamed to sub-stations sited in Australia, Brazil, China, Denmark, India and South Africa.

Nevada is also the site of Nuclear City, the world's foremost nuclear processing plant where fuel elements and atomic power cells are processed and manufactured. Nuclear City additionally supplies components and atomic fuel elements for compact nuclear devices that can be used as a source of portable energy at construction sites around the world, and manufactures power plants for various means of transport including aircraft and ships. The new World Air Force Goliath is one such craft, the strato-bomber requiring a high yield reactor to power its revolutionary anti-aircraft missile force field. Another is the recently launched Trans Pacific Shipping Corporation's ocean-going cruise ship the *President Roberts*, the biggest, fastest and most luxurious atomic pleasure liner in the world.

The provision of more conventional means of transportation is another of the World Government's principal responsibilities. Passenger aircraft remain one of the most common means of global travel, and intercontinental connections are now fully integrated with the construction of super-hub airports around the world, including those at New York, London, Paris, Novena in Italy, Shannon in Ireland, and the world's most widely used terminal, Boston's Atlantic airport. These are now served by a range of passenger aircraft, the largest of which are Intercontinental Airlines' fleet of cargo passenger strato-jets.

Terrestrial transport has been similarly revolutionised in recent years, on land and at sea. Long- and short-distance hover ferries provide smooth and quiet links between international and national ports, and the growth of the linear motor-powered monorail network has seen journey times cut significantly between the world's largest cities. Road transport has also benefited from a programme of super-highway construction with the aid of World Government funding, but with the majority of travellers now using other transport systems, road usage is now at a minimum.

World Government policies have also seen a worldwide improvement in health and the quality of life under the administration of the World Medical Organisation. New advances in preventative medicine have been developed by Manchester's Biological Research Centre in England and the Maryland Bacteriological Center in America, which have isolated and wiped out many diseases, while advances in brain surgery techniques have been introduced in London, through the use of a cerebral pulsator which reduces the risk of cortex trauma during operations. New research in to

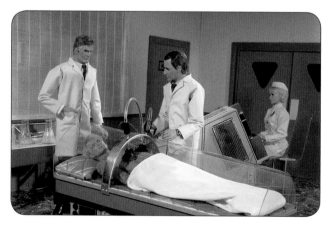

the unconscious mind has now resulted in the discovery of a means of artificially inducing a state of sleep which can enable the body to perform at a higher degree of physical efficiency when re-awoken, and following extensive clinical trials at Canada's Slaton hospital, a process has been developed to resuscitate a patient after expiration.

Cultural welfare is seen as another important aspect of World Government policy and has resulted in the foundation of the World Cultural Council, an international body responsible for bringing traditional and modern forms of artistic expression to the widest possible audience. Presenting regular showcases of the arts at international venues, the most prestigious of which will be the forthcoming World Cultural Congress to be held at Ireland's newly constructed Athlone Entertainments Complex, the council is currently headed by the charismatic Russian Dr Brodski, formerly director of the Moscow Institute of People's Music. Other projects supported by the council include the TeleVisual Radio network of manned satellites which provide 24-hour news and entertainment channels to the world's population, and innovative public buildings such as the newly constructed 800 foot high Car-Vue skypark in North Hampshire, England, which offers unparallel views of the country's capital and south coast. The council is also currently developing the Expo 2068 site in Canada for completion later this year, which will showcase the latest international achievements in science and technology.

Other than civilian planetary concerns, the World Government is looking beyond the earth to develop a co-ordinated civilian and military presence in space, an ambition which has already led to the initial colonisation of the Moon, while in both spheres the formation of centrally controlled military organisations has led to a cohesive structure for global defence against hostile elements, including World Government non-member states. Working closely with military forces and under the overall authority of the World Security Council, the World Police from its headquarters in Paris, the World Government Police Corps and World Government-authorised security services are similarly tasked with ensuring the population of the planet is protected from potential threats. A recent radical overhaul of security services has seen former national and international covert intelligence organisations including the Australian-based Federal Agents Bureau and America's World Intelligence Network amalgamated into the Universal Security Service, so named due to its remit to engage with security concerns beyond the bounds of the Earth. Local security issues remain the responsibility of regional area intelligence services however, which play a vital role in monitoring specific national concerns.

With the new security arrangements finally in place a computer report was prepared for the World Security Council to identify any potential remaining weaknesses in the services being provided to maintain world stability. A significant conclusion of the report recognised that there was still a need for a highly progressive elite force that would provide a rapid response to deal with any incidents requiring immediate and expert attention. Answerable directly to the World President, the organisation would operate on a global basis and be capable of handling any aspect of security. Acting immediately on the report's recommendations the World Government authorised the creation of the new service, which to reflect the wide-ranging scope of its activities, was named Spectrum.

Forged with the utmost efficiency into a reality within a few short years, Spectrum became formally recognised with the granting of its official charter by the World President on 10 July 2067, and began to carry out the duties for which it was conceived. Circumstances would however soon dictate that the rationale for which it was originally created would be transformed by events on the planet Mars into a new and vital purpose. For reasons still shrouded in a high degree of mystery, the Earth had unexpectedly become engaged in a battle for survival against a mysterious alien force - a battle in which Spectrum is now at the forefront.

SPECTRUM IS GREEN

When plans for the formation of Spectrum were first drawn up, it was proposed that the organisation would be spearheaded by a team of experienced field agents under the control of a senior commanding officer, and that it would operate from a base that would also serve as a launch platform for a flight of advanced fighter aircraft. The organisation would also be able to call on a global network of resources that would include specially designed transport and fully equipped support bases.

In keeping with the name selected for the new service, every senior field officer would be assigned a colour coded rank. The commander-in-chief would be given the title Colonel White, and field agents would be led by a senior officer code-named Captain Black. Based on a series of psychological profiling tests, proving the suitability of female pilots for operating a newly developed control system, five female crew members would also be recruited to fly the organisation's flight of escort and strike aircraft. Both pilots and craft would be designated as Angels, with each pilot also being accorded a personal code-name. Within weeks of the decision being made to form Spectrum, recruitment began under the supervision of a World Government committee that included key members of the World Security Council. One

man immediately caught their attention as the ideal candidate to become commander-in-chief - former World Navy officer Charles Gray. Joining the committee, Gray would be personally involved with selecting the best candidates available to act as field agents and pilots, to be chosen primarily from world military and security services. Added to their ranks would be a top medical specialist, a communications officer, and a two-man senior research and development team.

Detailed proposals were then put forward to specify the practical resources that the organisation would be able to draw on. A fully self-sufficient base, capable of remaining operational for lengthy periods of time was a first consideration. After several alternative proposals were abandoned, an aerial platform equipped with a catapult flight deck for the Angel fighters was deemed the most practical solution. Given the name Cloudbase, the giant craft would provide accommodation for 600 crew and act as Spectrum's communication, command and conference centre.

In addition to the Angel aircraft, Spectrum would also be supplied with a fleet of passenger jets for long distance travel, and these, together with general purpose helicopters designed to meet short range needs, would be operated from affiliated

military bases around the world. In coastal sectors or in areas of rough terrain, bases would be further able to provide hovercraft transportation, while seaborne support would be offered by a small armada of submarines.

On the ground, field agents would find further means of transport available for their use including high speed patrol cars, VIP transport, mobile detector trucks and a network of armoured pursuit vehicles. They would also be able to call on support services and staff based in major cities to assist in security operations, and the skills of a variety of specialised agencies specifically created to ensure Spectrum's smooth day to day operational efficiency.

Over the following two years the organisation quickly took shape, its fully operational status being recognised in July 2067 with the granting of its official charter. Initially the formation and development of Spectrum was kept a closely guarded secret, with the construction of bases and resources carried out under strict security conditions. Soon however it became impossible to maintain total secrecy of the organisation's activities as the world's media became aware of certain aspects of its global presence. A training programme for the Angel flight in initially unmarked aircraft soon attracted attention in aviation circles while, as expected, the launch of Spectrum's newly constructed aerial platform did not go unnoticed. A series of press and publicity events were organised, including a display by the Angels at the Kentucky Air Show in April 2067 and culminated in an exclusive visit to Cloudbase by one of the world's leading journalists the following September.

Now the world would learn more about Spectrum, its command structure, and the role it would play in maintaining world security. Personally answerable to World President Younger, the well respected Colonel White controls Spectrum from a command centre based in the 'bridge' of Cloudbase. Here, with the assistance of communications officer Lieutenant Green, he can oversee all Spectrum operations from his rotating command desk. This enables him to maintain direct contact with field agents anywhere in the world, and with the Angel flight. A viewing screen connected to a global network of security cameras and a satellite surveillance map links him to every corner of the Earth, while Lieutenant Green operates his own computer console which gives him instant access to all Spectrum's information and communication systems.

Having received a call for action White can mobilise his team of field agents, initially led by Captain Black, who are on a rotating duty roster ready to be sent into action at a moment's notice from their standby lounge. From here they can be sent to deal with a security incident anywhere in the world by means of a Spectrum Passenger Jet. If necessary an Angel flight of three aircraft can also be launched in seconds for combat, search or

SPECTRUM CODE NAME :
Colonel White
OPERATIONAL DUTIES :
Commander-in-Chief
REAL NAME :
Charles Gray
DATE OF BIRTH :
14 July 2017
PLACE OF BIRTH :
London, England

BACKGROUND : Educated at King's College Canterbury and Norwich University. Graduated with degrees in computer control, navigation and technology. Volunteered for service with the World Navy and rose rapidly through the ranks to become commander of World Navy destroyer. Further promotion to youngest ever Admiral of the Fleet followed by resignation in 2047 to become naval liaison officer for World Intelligence Network. Appointed head of newly re-formed British section in 2052 with task of turning failing infiltration-ridden unit into efficient and trusted service. Successful resolution resulted in his remaining head of section until formation of Universal Secret Service in early 2060s. Expected to become USS director but instead accepted entirely new challenge – as Supreme Commander-in-Chief of the newly formed Spectrum Organisation.

PERSONAL INTERESTS : Reflecting his aptitude for strategic thinking, leisure pursuits include war games and writing detective fiction.

escort duty, with one aircraft permanently crewed for immediate launch on the flight deck and two further pilots ready in their own standby lounge - the Amber Room - to be elevated into their aircraft by means of a pressurised hydraulic lift system.

Once engaged in action on Earth's surface, field agents can be allocated one of the organisation's distinctive red saloon cars, a short-range helicopter or a hovercraft for general transportation. If a VIP is to be escorted under Spectrum's protection, a bomb and guided missile resistant Maximum Security vehicle can be utilised, or a 'Yellow Fox' mobile conference centre camouflaged as a fuel tanker. For greater operational versatility in potentially hazardous missions, field agents are also authorised to requisition a Spectrum Pursuit Vehicle, a high speed multi-purpose armoured car. Due to the heavy armaments installed in the vehicle, SPV's are stationed in secret storage facilities located in strategic positions around the world - each manned by a local Spectrum agent. Adding to its versatility the SPV is fitted with a detachable power unit which can be used to operate a variety of equipment stored in the vehicle including a one-man thruster pack. Other vehicles available for field use include Detector Trucks equipped with Geiger counters capable

of locating radioactive materials and six Clam class submarines constantly patrolling the world's oceans. Spectrum agents can also call on any World Government military service vehicle that might prove essential for a particular mission.

Further specialised equipment that might be required for operational use can be supplied by Spectrum ground forces, notably special weapons and clothing. These include colour-coded thermally heated leather jackets for sub-zero weather conditions, lightweight safari suits for equatorial zones, flight wear for airborne duties and space suits. Like the impact-resistant suede tunic uniforms worn by senior officers and the Angel's elegant cream flying suits this apparel, together with other work wear worn by Spectrum personnel, was designed by the Parisian couturier the House of Verdain.

An integral part of the officers' uniform and the Angels' flying suits are the high powered transmitter/receivers respectively built into the officers' caps and the Angels' helmets. These allow the wearers to make direct contact with operatives and with Colonel White at his control desk. As part of operational procedure Spectrum has also introduced specific verbal acknowledgements to indicate mission status. The phrases used are 'Spectrum is Green', when a situation is under control and a course of action is proceeding to plan, or 'Spectrum is Red' to indicate an emergency or when severe difficulties have arisen.

To ensure that full radio contact can be maintained at all times, Spectrum has launched is own network of relay and booster satellites, designed to provide the organisation with the best communication system in the world. This communication system would however play a key part in triggering a series of events that would dramatically change the role of Spectrum, leading it into a conflict that would threaten the existence of Earth and its inhabitants. Having been fitted with receivers tuned to pick up signals from deep space, the system confirmed the broadcast of transmissions from an area of Mars that had initially been detected following the return of the first successful manned expedition to the planet. To investigate whether these transmissions could pose any threat to Earth, Colonel White assigned Captain Black to lead a new mission to the planet aboard a Zero X spacecraft. Launched in late 2067, the expedition made planet-fall in early 2068 and proceeded to survey the target area. After a last report that their surveys had so far proved inconclusive, all contact with the crew was lost.

It was not until some six weeks later that an explanation for this loss of contact became known. Having lost hope of ever discovering the fate of the expedition, authorities on Earth were astonished when tracking stations detected the Zero X main body taking up position in Earth orbit according to landing procedure. Despite the continued lack of radio contact, lifting bodies were launched and successfully reconnected with the main

body under onboard control. The craft then proceeded to make a textbook approach to its landing strip at Glenn Field spaceport.

Immediately alerted by the World Solar Space Command that Captain Black's expedition was returning to Earth, Colonel White flew at once to Glenn Field, but his flight was tracked by a newsman aboard another aircraft who had learnt of a possible breaking story involving Spectrum. In the skies above Glenn Field a mid-air collision occurred when the newsman's aircraft clipped the returning Zero X, and in the confusion that followed nobody sighted Captain Black slipping away from the main body of Zero X. Only on later viewing of security camera recordings that took place following the discovery that the excursion vehicle had returned crewless to its standby station, was he seen leaving the spaceport in a motor pool saloon.

Subsequent examination of the Zero X flight recorder revealed the circumstances that preceded Captain Black's inexplicable behaviour. While making a final survey of the Martian surface the crew of the MEV had discovered an incredible alien complex from which it appeared the signals received by Spectrum had emanated. In an uncharacteristic act of panic, Captain Black then ordered a missile attack on the complex, resulting in its complete devastation. A message transmitted to the crew was then heard for the first time by Colonel White and the assembled officials, accompanying images recorded on camera demonstrating the senders' powers. As the alien buildings were reconstructed before their astonished eyes, it tonelessly stated - *'Earthmen - we are peaceful beings and you have tried to destroy us. But you cannot succeed. You and your people will pay for this act of aggression. This is the voice of the Mysterons. We know that you can hear us Earthmen. Our retaliation will be slow, but nonetheless effective. It will mean the ultimate destruction of life on Earth. It will be useless for you to resist for we have discovered the secret of recreating matter as you have just witnessed. One of you will be under our control. You will be instrumental in avenging the Mysterons. Our first act of retaliation will be to assassinate your World President.'* At this point all flight records ceased.

On viewing the flight recording and having learnt that a potential assassin in the form of Captain Black was now at large, Colonel White returned at once to Cloudbase. From here he would supervise plans to ensure the World President's safety, and having first briefed them fully with details of the events on Mars, assigned leading field agents Captain Scarlet and Captain Brown to supervise local security and escort the president to the Spectrum Maximum Security building in New York.

During the course of their mission it was discovered that both Captain Brown and Captain Scarlet had been killed as a result of a car crash and replaced with Mysteron replicas. After one unsuccessful assassination attempt by the replica Captain Brown, the World President was then kidnapped by Captain Scarlet and

taken to a Mysteron rendezvous at the London Car-vue sky park. Already in the country to review security, Captain Blue was alerted to Scarlet's actions and proceeded at speed to the sky-park in a requisitioned SPV. Spectrum helicopter A42, stationed at Boscombe Air Base was also despatched to the area to provide mission support, but as the later discovery of wreckage in the Boscombe area substantiated, somehow the vehicle had been sabotaged and substituted with a Mysteron reconstruction.

Events at the sky-park further appeared to indicate a change in the Mysterons' intentions, which according to sono-detector recordings made of Mysteron transmissions made in the area at the time instructed Scarlet to hold the president hostage rather than carry out the threat of assassination. An Angel air strike ordered against the helicopter then resulted in catastrophic disaster when the stricken craft collided with the sky-park ramp-way. With the aid of the SPV thruster pack, Captain Blue successfully airlifted the president to safety, but the Mysteronised Scarlet plunged 800 feet to the ground below, a fall that would have meant death for an ordinary man.

Having retrieved Scarlet's body, a Spectrum medical team arranged to have it flown back to Cloudbase in the hope that it would reveal information about the Mysteron process of retro-metabolism, but on arrival Spectrum's chief medical officer Dr Fawn was astonished to find that the captain was now showing signs of life, and that his wounds were healing. With the aid of a specially developed computer of his own design, Fawn was able to reverse the Mysterons' control over their reconstruction, allowing it to regain Scarlet's dormant original personality. Even more miraculously, comprehensive tests showed that the revived Scarlet had retained the mysterious powers of retro-metabolism, enabling him to recover from any wounds or injuries. After extensive physical and psychological examination Scarlet was declared fit to return to active duty and has now proved himself in countless missions to be Spectrum's most formidable weapon in the fight against the Mysterons.

CLOUDBASE

Stationed at 40,000 feet above the Earth, Spectrum's carrier platform Cloudbase serves as the organisation's operational headquarters and command centre. It is from here that all Spectrum's missions are controlled.

Cloudbase
Technical data

LENGTH:	630ft
WIDTH:	330ft
WEIGHT:	4,520,000lbs
RANGE:	unlimited
LOCATION:	variable
STANDARD OPERATIONAL CEILING:	40,000ft

PRIMARY DATAFILE

After several alternative proposals including a super-submarine, a floating island and a remote land-based location were rejected, the proposal to base Spectrum's command centre aboard an airborne carrier craft was unanimously approved by the World Security Council. A miracle of 21st-century technology, Cloudbase was initially built in sections on Earth at a World Government facility in Stockholm before being transferred piece by piece to be assembled in space by a crew based at an abandoned weather satellite.

Once completed, its nuclear reactor was programmed for activation and the immense craft was manoeuvred into the Earth's atmosphere to take up a holding position at 40,000 feet with the aid of anti-gravity compensators and four powerful hover combines.

Split into two main sections, the main body of the craft forms a giant airstrip in the sky, enabling conventional aircraft, helijets and helicopters to take off and land, while an additional catapult flight deck serves as a launch facility for Spectrum's squadron of Angel Interceptor fighters. Within the main body of the craft are housed the power units and life support systems, accommodation for maintenance crew and ancillary staff, a medical centre, workshops, and two aircraft hangars.

The other principal section of the carrier, linked by connecting supports to one pair of hover combines is the command centre. From here Spectrum's Commander-in-Chief Colonel White can control all of Spectrum's operations with the aid of his communications officer Lieutenant Green. This section of the craft also provides accommodation and living quarters for Spectrum's senior field officers and Angel pilots, in addition to information and observation control rooms.

Power for the carrier is primarily supplied by a nuclear fusion reactor. This is supplemented by solar panels that generate energy for heat, light and life support systems. Additional power for the hover combines is available through the jet cloud conversion engines fitted to each unit which can also be utilised to move Cloudbase from one area of the world to another.

BACKGROUND : Graduated from Kingston University with degrees in telecommunications, technology and music. Enrolled with newly formed World Aquanaut Security Patrol to carry out land-based WASP communication duties, becoming controller of tele-relay systems at newly constructed service headquarters at Marineville. Later transferred to undersea duties, seeing active service as submarine hydrophones operator in actions carried out to investigate rumours of hostile undersea races. Following formation of Spectrum accepted post of chief communications officer. Instrumental in designing and installing communication and deep-space transmission receivers aboard Spectrum satellite communication network.

PERSONAL INTERESTS : Accomplished musician and singer specialising in traditional West Indian music.

Designed to create an efficient and comfortable environment for its officers and crew, the work stations, living quarters and recreational zones aboard Cloudbase make optimum use of all the available internal space.

CREW FACILITIES

A virtual city in the sky, Cloudbase is home to almost 600 men and women, and is equipped to remain self-sufficient for long periods of time. Aboard can be found all the amenities required to maximise mission efficiency and cater for the on and off duty needs of its crew, every effort having been made to alleviate the isolation of the craft's remote position through the facilities incorporated.

Almost as if it were a giant living creature, Cloudbase is divided into two main sections – the head, or command centre, and the main body. In the Command Centre can be found all the control systems central to the carrier's operation, with its control room acting as the craft's nerve centre, while the main body houses the 'heart' of the ship, the compact fusion reactor. In a similar manner the rigorously selected and trained officers and crew of Cloudbase could be described as its life blood and the need to maintain their physical and psychological well being is deemed of paramount importance to ensure the ship's smooth running and the effective deployment of its officers and resources.

SPECTRUM CODE NAME :
Doctor Fawn
OPERATIONAL DUTIES :
Chief Medical Officer
REAL NAME :
Edward Wilkie
DATE OF BIRTH :
10 July 2031
PLACE OF BIRTH :
Yalumba, Australia

BACKGROUND : Son of a renowned medical specialist and honours graduate of Brisbane University in biology and medicine. Appointed assistant controller of World Medical Organisation Australian sector on completion of studies. Recognised growing need to modernise service and developed plans for re-organisation following promotion to health controller of Scandinavian section. Within two years had formulated revolutionary system to introduce robot doctors equipped with x-ray eyes capable of nano-speed diagnosis. Offered position of administrator for the advancement of medicine with resources to implement proposals. Spectrum selection committee recognised his outstanding ability and invited him to become the organisation's medical officer.

PERSONAL INTERESTS : Devotes spare time to continued development of robot medical techniques.

If the Command Centre can be regarded as the craft's 'head', then its 'brains' must be the complex banks of computers and information systems housed on the upper deck. Here can be found the ship's control room, an imaginatively designed space from which Colonel White commands Spectrum operations while seated at a rotating circular control desk. This allows him to view mission activities on a large multi-purpose screen, or alternatively confer with senior officers who can be offered elevating seating which surrounds the desk. Also located in the control room is Lieutenant Green's communications console, a single solid plasma unit which Green operates from a moving control chair which runs along the length of the unit.

Elsewhere on this deck of the Command Centre can be found the Spectrum Information Centre and the Spectrum Observation Room which can supply the latest information and visual reports from around the world. In this section of Cloudbase are also located a conference room, officers' quarters and standby lounge, a swimming pool, a promenade deck and two observation tubes offering views of the skies around Cloudbase.

Below the Command Centre, and accessed by high speed escalators housed in the centre's two support arms, are the workshops and control rooms needed to support the carrier's power sources, life support systems and stationed aircraft, with offices, accommodation and facilities for the ship's crew, including sports courts, a cinema and the Cloudbase Medical Centre. Beneath the catapult flight deck for the Angel aircraft can also be found the Amber Room, the Angel crew's tastefully designed standby lounge.

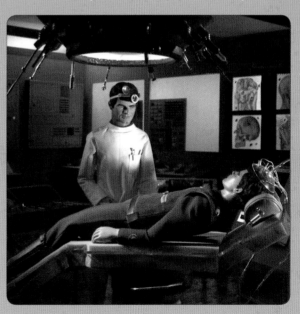

CLOUDBASE: OVERVIEW

Spectrum's airborne carrier Cloudbase serves as the organisation's command headquarters and the launch pad for its fleet of supersonic Angel Interceptor fighters.

Cloudbase: overview

1 Cloudbase Command Centre

2 Medical bay located under flight deck

3 Helicopter landing pad primarily used by medical personnel with close access to adjacent medical bay

4 Gymnasium

5 Changing rooms

6 Lecture theatre and conference centre

7 Seminar room

8 Crew quarters

9 Nuclear fusion reactor provides the primary source of power for Cloudbase, mainly supplying energy to the four hover combines and the anti-gravity generators, alongside solar-energy panels which also power heat, light and life-support functions

10 Angel Interceptor landing ramps rise up 30 degrees to align with incoming aircraft using their VTOL jets and electro-magnets incorporated into their undercarriage

11 Hover combine turbofan provides down-draught ensuring Cloudbase remains level in all weather conditions, and operates in conjunction with anti-gravity generating systems

12 Jet cloud conversion engines provide additional power to the hover combine turbofan and can also move Cloudbase to a new location in conjunction with adjacent stabilising and directional jets

13 Twin stabilising and directional jets: used to relocate Cloudbase in the event of bad weather, or for strategic or maintenance operations

14 No.2 main hangar

15 Aircraft fuel tanks

16 Reactor excess heat bleed-off pipe valves control air temperature of the six heating tubes that run along the underside of Cloudbase

17 Air and atmosphere recycling tanks

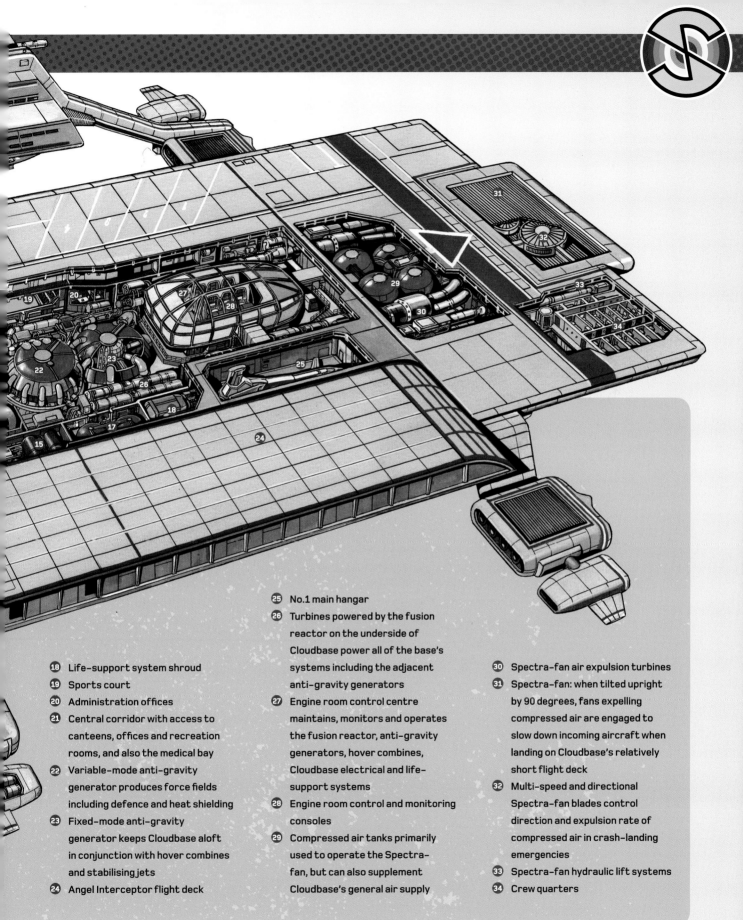

25 No.1 main hangar

26 Turbines powered by the fusion reactor on the underside of Cloudbase power all of the base's systems including the adjacent anti-gravity generators

27 Engine room control centre maintains, monitors and operates the fusion reactor, anti-gravity generators, hover combines, Cloudbase electrical and life-support systems

28 Engine room control and monitoring consoles

29 Compressed air tanks primarily used to operate the Spectra-fan, but can also supplement Cloudbase's general air supply

18 Life-support system shroud

19 Sports court

20 Administration offices

21 Central corridor with access to canteens, offices and recreation rooms, and also the medical bay

22 Variable-mode anti-gravity generator produces force fields including defence and heat shielding

23 Fixed-mode anti-gravity generator keeps Cloudbase aloft in conjunction with hover combines and stabilising jets

24 Angel Interceptor flight deck

30 Spectra-fan air expulsion turbines

31 Spectra-fan: when tilted upright by 90 degrees, fans expelling compressed air are engaged to slow down incoming aircraft when landing on Cloudbase's relatively short flight deck

32 Multi-speed and directional Spectra-fan blades control direction and expulsion rate of compressed air in crash-landing emergencies

33 Spectra-fan hydraulic lift systems

34 Crew quarters

The Command Centre of Cloudbase is Spectrum's operational nerve centre, and houses the craft's control room, computer banks, communication systems and officers' quarters.

Cloudbase: Command Centre

1 Control room featuring the Cloudbase computer manned by Lieutenant Green, and Colonel White's revolving control console. Behind the console is an LCD screen on which diagrams, graphics and video images from the Spectrum Information Centre can be displayed

2 Observation tube

3 Service ducts provide space for Cloudbase's electronics, plumbing and heating services

4 Conference room

5 Spectrum Information Centre, incorporating seventh-generation supercomputers and plasma data-storage systems

6 Helipad access airlock

7 Helipad

8 Observation room, from which information can be relayed to Lt Green's console and to the Spectrum Information Centre

9 Central lift to all decks

10 Promenade deck

11 Foam and fire-retardant chemical storage tanks: in the event of a fire, chemicals can be pumped to anywhere in the base via Cloudbase's extensive piping system

12 Officers' restaurant

13 Library

14 Stairs and escalators link command centre with Cloudbase flight deck via an access passage within the adjacent hover combines

15 Access 'landing' to other decks

16 Support stanchion incorporates air conditioning, service ducts and steam pipes providing heat from flight deck solar panels

17 Officers' sleeping quarters: the Room of Sleep is located in an adjacent area on this level

18 Officers' lounge

19 Communications and media console provides world TV reception, newspaper and magazine print-outs, and computer facilities

20 Swimming pool

21 Swimming pool changing and shower rooms

22 Spectrum officers' cabins; a system of mirrors and prisms in each room reflects natural light from the six central windows

23 Spectrum communications room handles day to day communications links between Cloudbase and Spectrum bases, agents and associated ground personnel, who maintain vehicles and aircraft all over the world

24 Communications antenna

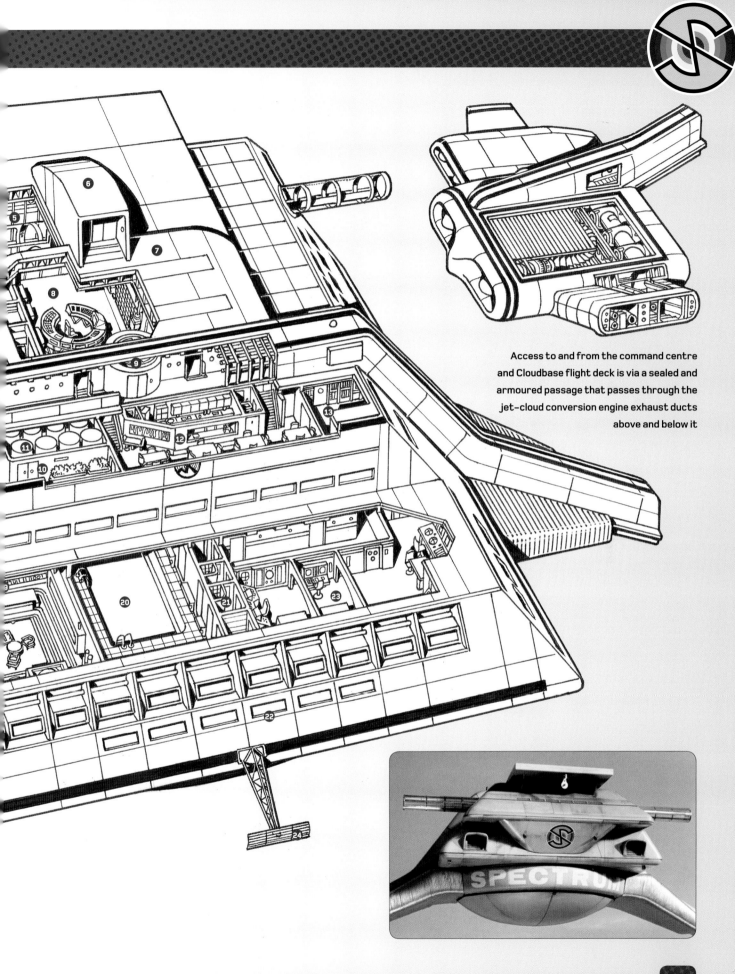

Access to and from the command centre and Cloudbase flight deck is via a sealed and armoured passage that passes through the jet–cloud conversion engine exhaust ducts above and below it

CLOUDBASE: FLIGHT DECK

The main body of Cloudbase forms the carrier's flight deck and houses power and life support systems in addition to aircraft hangars and workshops. A separate catapult launch deck is provided for Spectrum's flight of Angel Interceptors.

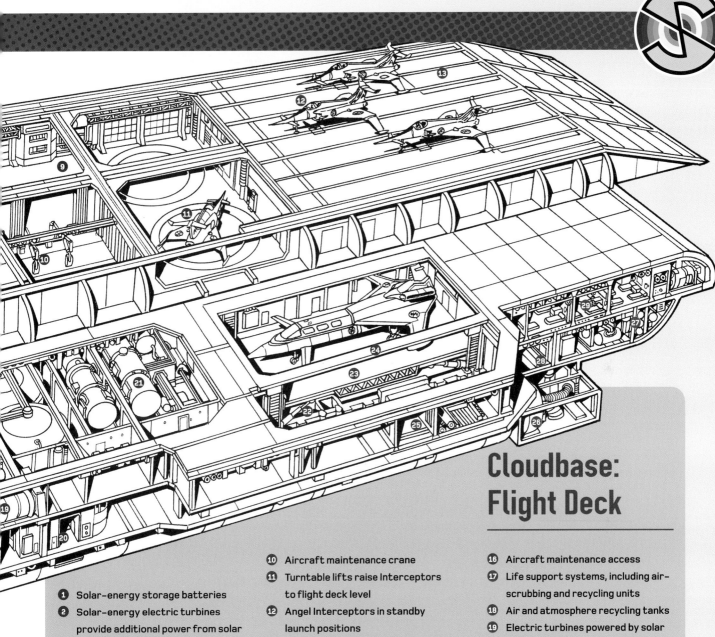

Cloudbase: Flight Deck

1. Solar-energy storage batteries
2. Solar-energy electric turbines provide additional power from solar panels around the perimeter of Cloudbase
3. Processed filtered exhaust outlets
4. Aircraft component repair, storage and manufacturing unit
5. Angel Interceptor exhaust processing and disposal unit
6. Angel Interceptor testing bay
7. Aircraft maintenance workshop
8. Aircraft maintenance control rooms and workshops
9. Interceptor general maintenance and cleaning bay: large hangars ensure there is plenty of room for technicians to service the aircraft
10. Aircraft maintenance crane
11. Turntable lifts raise Interceptors to flight deck level
12. Angel Interceptors in standby launch positions
13. Angel Interceptor landing ramps: using their centrally mounted VTOL jet, Interceptors can land quickly, coming to an immediate halt using landing ramps that raise 30 degrees to electromagnetically clamp the aircraft undercarriage to the flight deck take-off grooves
14. Underside heating tubes, along with solar panels and heat-conducting runway surface technologies prevent Cloudbase from freezing at high altitudes
15. No.1 main hangar, used for other Spectrum aircraft, such as passenger jets or helicopters
16. Aircraft maintenance access
17. Life support systems, including air-scrubbing and recycling units
18. Air and atmosphere recycling tanks
19. Electric turbines powered by solar energy and the adjacent fusion reactor provide heat, light and power for all Cloudbase functions, including life support
20. Laboratories and workshops
21. Aircraft fixed storage tanks
22. Hangar lift hydraulics
23. No.2 main hangar, used by Spectrum craft other than Interceptors
24. Pressurised hangar door
25. Hangar personnel entrance
26. Processed waste-disposal filters
27. Water pipes, heating and auto-repair system conduits
28. Staff shop
29. Maintenance crew quarters

CLOUDBASE: MEDICAL CENTRE

Equipped for any emergency eventuality, the Cloudbase Medical Centre incorporates the latest medical technology including Auto-Doc diagnostic and treatment systems and anti-radiation decontamination units.

Cloudbase: Medical Centre

1. General recovery ward
2. Ceiling-mounted privacy screen
3. Laundry
4. Medical bay food preparation unit
5. Toilet and shower room
6. Treatment rooms
7. MRI scanning room
8. Treatment spa
9. Nurses' living quarters
10. Nurses' sleeping quarters
11. Shower and toilet
12. Decontamination unit
13. Doctor Fawn's office
14. Cloudbase and Spectrum medical data files
15. Women's ward
16. Duty nurse's station
17. Medical supplies store
18. Bathroom and toilet
19. Outpatient's surgery
20. Men's ward
21. Duty nurse's station
22. Equipment store
23. Toilet
24. Outpatients' waiting room
25. Outpatients' reception
26. Main reception desk
27. Linen store
28. Standby operating theatre
29. Decontamination unit
30. No.1 main operating theatre
31. Life recovery unit
32. MRI scanner
33. Scanner operators' suite
34. Isolation room and monitor/scanner

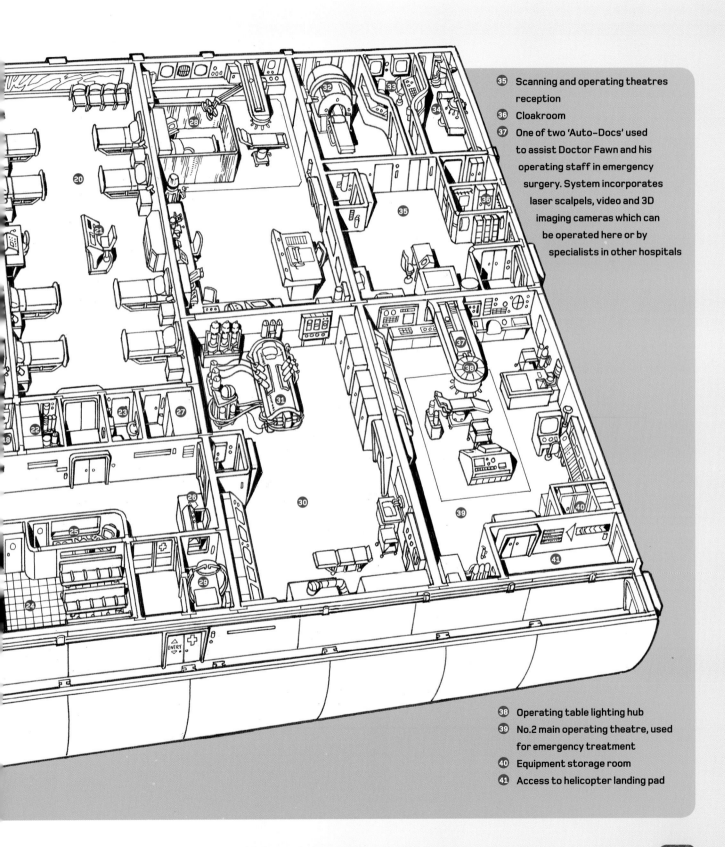

35 Scanning and operating theatres reception

36 Cloakroom

37 One of two 'Auto-Docs' used to assist Doctor Fawn and his operating staff in emergency surgery. System incorporates laser scalpels, video and 3D imaging cameras which can be operated here or by specialists in other hospitals

38 Operating table lighting hub

39 No.2 main operating theatre, used for emergency treatment

40 Equipment storage room

41 Access to helicopter landing pad

THIS IS SPECTRUM

When the decision to form Spectrum was first approved by the World Government, the immense logistical challenge soon became apparent. The new organisation would require a massive investment in men, women and technology. Drawing initially on the ranks of the World Government's armed forces, recruitment of essential staff to supervise the establishment of a network of construction and support services began immediately. Where possible the best existing military and civilian hardware would be adapted and modified to serve Spectrum's needs, while new designs were swiftly drawn up and computer assessed to create blueprints for other essential vehicles and craft. These would include Spectrum's entirely revolutionary control base which, following the dismissal of alternative proposals, was finally agreed would be a giant airborne carrier.

New and existing buildings were soon constructed or converted to provide regional command centres for support staff, and to house the chain of service and supply depots required for transport and equipment, all of which were vital to ensure the smooth running of the organisation., Plans were drawn up for a purpose-built office complex located to the West of London which would serve as Spectrum's supreme headquarters and were realised in record time to allow the building to become operational less than six months after the decision to form the organisation had been taken. From here Spectrum's newly selected Commander-in-Chief Charles Gray, under his Spectrum code name Colonel White, would supervise

the establishment of a worldwide network of administrative agencies responsible for serving Spectrum's specialised needs. At the same time he would also begin the rigorous process of selecting an elite team of senior field agents and aerial wing fighter pilots to lead Spectrum missions.

To maintain the security of the new organisation, planning and preparation to develop facilities and resources would be carried out in the utmost secrecy. All Spectrum command centres, storage depots and worldwide agencies would operate from dummy premises, under the guise of legitimate businesses, and supplies and components would be sourced and routed through seemingly innocent commercial concerns before reaching their intended destination. In this way it was hoped that any potential hostile elements would be deterred from sabotaging Spectrum's growing infrastructure.

Ultimate responsibility for overseeing this process, and for the creation of Spectrum's organisational framework would lie with Spectrum's Logistics Executive. This dedicated and highly trained team of efficiency specialists devised the roles each individual agency would play. Agencies responsible for the day to day running of Spectrum would include construction, supply and maintenance. Staffed by the most technically proficient personnel available, these agencies would be charged with overseeing the smooth and efficient implementation of Spectrum's global operational requirements.

Alongside these essential agencies, another of the earliest Spectrum sub-divisions to be granted official status by the Logistics Executive was the Spectrum Research and Development Agency. Under the guidance of the technically brilliant and inventive engineering genius Major Viridian, together with his aide, the Harvard-educated electronics wizard Lieutenant Cobalt, the challenge to create an effective and reliable fleet of vehicles and ancillary equipment for Spectrum's use was met with imaginative determination. The decision to adapt or modify existing civilian or military vehicles where possible, such as the Zeus tank, Viper fighter, the Rotar helicopter and Universal Aero's TVR 4 proved exceptionally successful, with additional vehicles being designed to factor practicality and ease of construction as foremost considerations.

Viridian also devised the innovative plan to build Spectrum's new sky platform headquarters in outer space using apparently innocent components that could be shipped to a central World Government depot in Sweden and then transported into orbit from Siberia's international space freight base to a disused weather satellite. In a similar manner he introduced the method whereby unmodified military vehicles, such as the Viper fighter built by International Engineering's Fairfield Aviation subsidiary in England, would be delivered by road freighter to

remote warehouse units from which they would be collected by authorised Spectrum transporters and conveyed to final assembly plants for the fitting of specialised equipment.

While development proceeded with the design and construction of facilities and transport, a further Spectrum Agency – Communications – was set the challenge of creating a new and secure system that would enable the various sections of the organisation to maintain instant and unmonitorable contact around the world. To achieve this a network of relay and booster station satellites were launched into orbit to amplify all ground signals and give Spectrum complete global coverage. Receivers on the satellites were also directed towards outer space, to boost the chances of picking up signals from elsewhere in the Solar System – particularly those which had been detected as emanating from the planet Mars.

It soon became clear that maintaining the secret nature of Spectrum's activities would require the creation of a unit specifically responsible for carrying out this task. As a result the Spectrum Covert Operations Agency was formed. Employing some of the world's most creative minds, this small but vitally important part of Spectrum would be engaged in devising inventive and convincing ways to conceal Spectrum's presence around the world. One of their greatest challenges

was to conceive unusual and unexpected locations in which to base Spectrum's fleet of armoured pursuit vehicles that would make them easily accessible for use by field agents. Responsibility for manning these hidden requisition posts would be given to highly skilled undercover agents who would be able to blend in with the surrounding community without arousing suspicion, while possessing the expertise to maintain the SPV in full mission readiness.

Further support for the organisation's operations would be provided by Spectrum Ground Forces. These multi-skilled teams have been trained to work in conjunction with local security units found in every major city to provide personnel capable of undertaking field operations such as area searches and the manning of checkpoints and roadblocks, for which they are able to utilise locally based fleets of patrol cars and detector vans. Spectrum Ground Forces are further equipped to carry out search and rescue missions in the event that any Spectrum operatives might be reported missing in action. Their units also frequently find themselves working with the Spectrum Police, a specially trained corps of officers responsible for the organisation's internal security and for local and international police liaison in the event of suspected criminal activity, or the implementation of public order measures such as mass evacuations. Mobile units of armed guards from the Spectrum Security Agency can also be called on to support specific security alerts in addition to their duties to maintain constant surveillance over key Spectrum buildings and installations, among the most strongly guarded of which are those concerned with records, fuel supply and VIP protection. Even before the recent changes to the nature of Spectrum's official security role, round-the-clock watches have been in place at all such sites to counter possible intrusion by undesirables or the potential consequences of enemy action.

With the establishment of the Spectrum Records Agency, a vital source of computerised information available to Spectrum

operatives, the need for a secure archive was recognised. Situated on the North East coast of the United States, near Portland, Maine, Spectrum maintains the Spectrum Security Vault, a highly advanced storage facility designed to fulfil this need. Equipped with one of the world's most impregnable strongrooms, the vault contains nothing of monetary value, but acts as a repository for hard copies of all Spectrum's records and operational reports, stored as a safeguard against the possible compromisation of computerised data. These sensitive documents include a full account of Spectrum's operational history and comprehensively detail all the organisation's global security commitments, including its most recent ultra-confidential planetary defence assignments.

Similar high security measures are constantly in force to protect Spectrum's fuel production and supply chain. All Spectrum's primary conventional fuel requirements are met by the output of the ultra-sonic deep wells and refinery complex at Bensheba in Arabia. Here the hyper-premium grade deposits are refined using various secret processes and additives, including Harrison long range economy enhancement synthesis and the Colboltibe high performance enhancer, in addition to standard aviation and diesel fuel production methods. To add to the security of Spectrum's fuel supply and distribution requirements, many of these are carried out under the auspices of the internationally available Delta fuel brand. Special watch has also been placed on other plants around the world producing hydrogenic and Alpha-grade fuel cells to ensure their unrestricted availability for use in Spectrum vehicles.

Perhaps the most purposefully guarded of all Spectrum's facilities are the maximum security structures situated around the world. These are designed to provide secure and self-contained accommodation and amenities for single and group VIP use. They can be centrally located, such as the New York Maximum Security Building, which offers subterranean reception and office space connected by elevators and moving

walkways, with access protected by defensive detector units, or built in open countryside, as evidenced by the Vandon Security Base and the European Maximum Security Centre. These provide secure underground bunkers surrounded by electronically controlled perimeter warning systems reinforced by dummy structural features in the event that external barriers might be breached. Security facilities can also be found in more remote areas, including central Africa, where a conference centre, designated Base Zebra, has been constructed in the centre of a game reserve and camouflaged behind the innocent façade of a hunting lodge. Forty checkpoints manned by Spectrum Security guards in the guise of game wardens form an impregnable ring around the lodge building, which at the turn of an electronic key in a control unit, can descend beneath the ground, delivering delegates to a fully equipped, soundproof conference suite. The importance of Base Zebra is underlined by its having been allocated a designated field officer, Captain Indigo, to ensure the smooth running of the site.

The task of running Spectrum is immense, and to ensure that the demands of maintaining its operational efficiency are met, training bases have been set up around the world under the control of the Spectrum Personnel Training Agency. Recruiting men and women from the best military and educational backgrounds, the Personnel Training Agency bases offer potential support staff and officer cadets the best academic and vocational skill-set development possible. Base Eagle, Base Dolphin, Base White Owl and Base Koala are just four of the Spectrum academies that operatives will pass through to gain experience of Spectrum's technological and practical resources.

In the light of recent events an increasingly important role is now being played by the most unobtrusive of all Spectrum's agencies, the Spectrum Intelligence Agency. The SIA, as it is informally known, is charged with gathering together and analysing all information that may optimise Spectrum's efficiency in dealing with any potential security challenge. This

role has now attained even greater importance due to the state of war that now exists between the Earth and the mysterious alien force known as the Mysterons. All the SIA's expertise has consequently been directed to countering any threatened retaliatory attacks through the gathering of intelligence and the monitoring of designated targets, while developing at the same time new and effective means of defeating the Mysterons.

To this end the newest, and possibly most vital of all Spectrum agencies has been formed to work in close collaboration with the Spectrum Research and Development Agency and the Spectrum Armoury. Under the direction of the SIA's chief of scientific research Dr Giardello, the Spectrum Special Weapons Agency has already developed a field-proven Mysteron detector and a short-range Mysteron gun. Tests are also now being carried out on a high powered Electro-ray rifle capable of eliminating Mysteron agents at long range. With such weapons and other methods continually being tested it is hoped that they may provide a means for Spectrum to combat any Mysteron threats until a permanent end to the existing war of nerves between Earth and the Mysterons can be found.

SPECTRUM PURSUIT VEHICLE

Spectrum's high powered armoured pursuit vehicle, the SPV has been designed to combine optimum speed pursuit duties with off-road versatility.

Spectrum Pursuit Vehicle
Technical data

LENGTH:	25ft
WIDTH:	8ft
TOP SPEED:	200mph (250mph on some versions)
TOP SPEED ON WATER:	50 knots

PRIMARY DATAFILE

Adapted from the World Army's semi-amphibious Zeus tank, the Spectrum Pursuit Vehicle was developed to provide multi-purpose transportation capable of coping with any potentially hazardous security incident. Substituting the Zeus tank's primary drive tracks with heavy duty main and secondary wheels, while retaining the original vehicle's subsidiary tracks, the SPV was radically redesigned internally to incorporate the pioneering concept of rear-facing driver and passenger seats. As the vehicle had already been configured to be controlled by external monitors this made little difference to its operation but considerably increased the crash protection offered to its occupants in the event of a collision.

Replacing the original engine unit, a newly designed dual function power system was installed which incorporated a removable power pack charged by fuel cells coupled with standby batteries to provide back-up power. Once removed the power pack could be used to provide energy for additional equipment, including a personal jet thruster. Primarily designed for one-man use, the thruster is powerful enough to lift a second person in the event of an emergency. Other tools that can be operated with the power pack include a high speed drill, a scuba jet, and a hoist. These additional fittings are stored in lockers with other useful equipment including a variety of weaponry, protective clothing and diving gear.

SPVs are stationed around the world in strategic positions and can be requisitioned from their camouflaged depots on production of an official Spectrum pass. In some locations SPVs have been stationed that have been built to retain the Zeus tank's amphibious capabilities and these have an operational number prefixed by the letter 'A'.

SPECTRUM CODE NAME :
Captain Scarlet
OPERATIONAL DUTIES :
Field Agent
REAL NAME :
Paul Metcalfe
DATE OF BIRTH :
17 December 2036
PLACE OF BIRTH :
Winchester, England

BACKGROUND : From a long-serving military family. Trained at West Point Military Academy. Following completion of degrees in technology, history and mathematical application at Winchester University joined World Army Air Force as private, rising rapidly to colonel through inspiring capacity to command and military professionalism. Having noted qualities of leadership, strategic thinking and dedication to duty, approached by Spectrum selection committee to become leading field agent. Commission accepted immediately.

SPECIAL NOTE : After reconstruction by Mysterons following death in car crash and subsequent fall from tall structure, replica accepted as serving officer having completed extensive tests revealing capacity for retro-metabolism and loss of Mysteron influence.

SPECTRUM PURSUIT VEHICLE

Incorporating a revolutionary monitor-controlled driving position and fitted with a forward-mounted high impact crash absorber, the SPV is engineered for maximum safety.

SPECTRUM PURSUIT VEHICLE: ARMAMENTS AND GUIDANCE SYSTEM

Spectrum Pursuit Vehicle

1. Starboard driver's position TV screens, electronics and TV camera output distribution box
2. Main computer monitors SPV systems diagnostics and external conditions data analysis
3. Upper arm extends port side seat and entry/exit hatch outwards to allow access to vehicle
4. Port side entry/exit hatch
5. Armourglass polarised viewpoint
6. Port side driver's seat: SPV can be driven from left- or right-hand driving positions
7. Ejection seat parachute pack
8. Hydrogenic fuel tank
9. Centrally mounted TV cameras located behind camouflaged armoured viewpoint, linked to driver's cabin video screens
10. Cannon door slot
11. Magazine and ammunition selector
12. Multi-function forward cannon can fire a variety of explosive shells, bullets and missiles
13. Forward cannon support and retraction brace: cannon can be held clear of the SPV and aimed precisely using underside turntable if required
14. Drive gears located in each of the larger wheels
15. Cantilevered drive support bracket
16. Drive support arm which pivots on the cantilevered bracket attached to the starboard shock absorber
17. Shock absorber
18. Forward shock absorber support brace
19. Headlights and TV camera
20. TV camera and starboard forward sensor electronics

21 Main hydraulic oil reservoir

22 Cahelium-strengthened tubular chassis

23 Fender and internal buoyancy tanks collapse in the event of a high-speed collision

24 Forward central buoyancy tanks used in amphibious operations

25 Bulldozer blade extends below fender to remove debris or snow in front of SPV if required

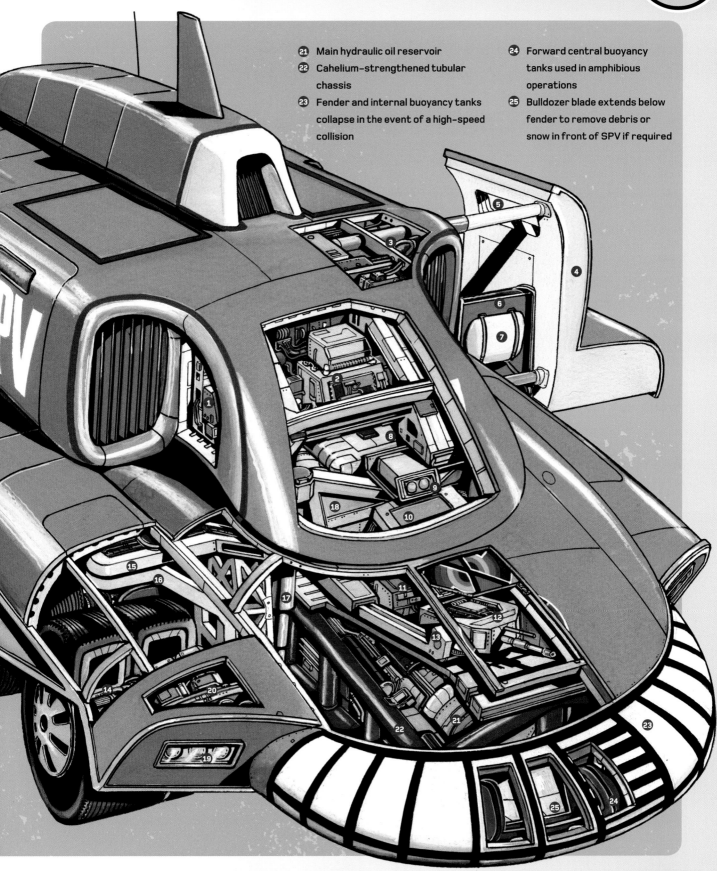

SPECTRUM PURSUIT VEHICLE

Capable of speeds in excess of 200mph the SPV is fitted with a removable power unit that can be installed in a portable thruster pack and other ancillary equipment.

SPECTRUM PURSUIT VEHICLE: INTERIOR AND PROPULSION

1. Emergency rear exit hatch
2. Rear TV camera
3. SPV inner bulkhead built around chassis keeps vehicle watertight
4. Heavy–duty caterpillar tracks, two on each cantilever
5. Secondary hydraulic jacks provide downwards force to maintain track adhesion in varying ground conditions
6. Rear track electric motor
7. Rear caterpillar track cantilever lowers track to wheel level to provide additional traction on rough, muddy or icy terrain
8. Cantilever hydraulic actuators
9. Starboard rear aquajet
10. Aquajet conversion unit
11. Buoyancy tanks built into mud flap/ fender underside, installed on 'A'– designation SPVs
12. Magnetic brakes
13. Hub and wheel gearing
14. Drive gears, located in each of the six larger wheels
15. Standby batteries operate SPV when power unit is in use elsewhere, installed within watertight enclosure
16. Water inlets and pump allow air to be pumped into SPV underside

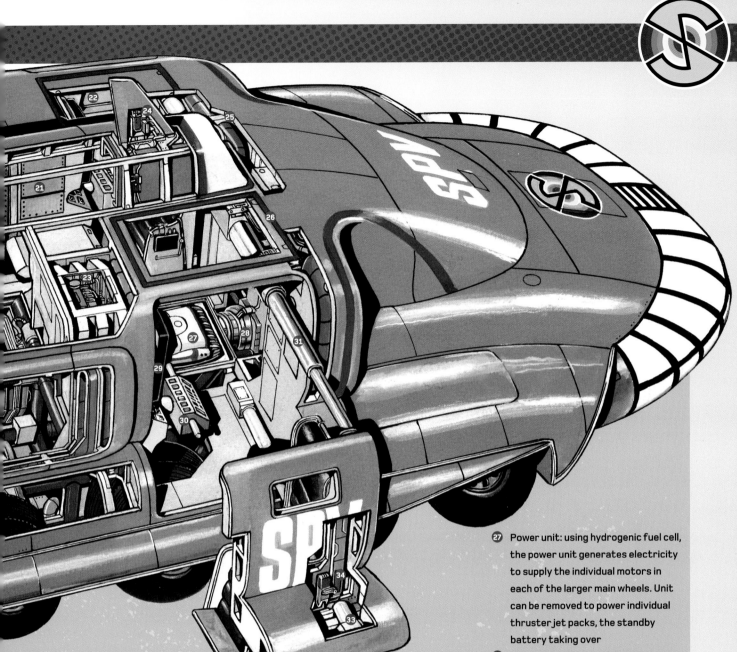

sealed units when SPV commences
amphibious operations

17 Central drawer-lined corridor

18 Drawer units along the vehicle's
central corridor contain food and
water supplies, tools, small arms and
folded uniforms/clothing for various
weather conditions

19 Thruster jet pack drawers contain
helmet and accessories to convert
power unit to flying mode; includes
bolt-on controls, straps and
directional compressor air jets

20 Air intake duct

21 Port side driver's console,
viewscreen and steering control
box

22 Exit hatch

23 Life-support system ensures
carbon dioxide is removed from
cabin using air-scrubbing systems

24 Topside external conditions sensors
built in to fin

25 Filtered power unit cooling duct

26 Ejection seat hatch

27 Power unit: using hydrogenic fuel cell,
the power unit generates electricity
to supply the individual motors in
each of the larger main wheels. Unit
can be removed to power individual
thruster jet packs, the standby
battery taking over

28 Forward turbine powers SPV using
electricity from standby batteries
when power unit is removed

29 Drivers' viewscreen displays images
from fore and aft cameras

30 Starboard steering column and
control box

31 Upper hatch support arm in extended
position

32 Starboard driver's seat, in partly
lowered position

33 Lower hatch support arm holding
door in extended position, allowing
seat to lower to ground level

34 Seat lowering hydraulics

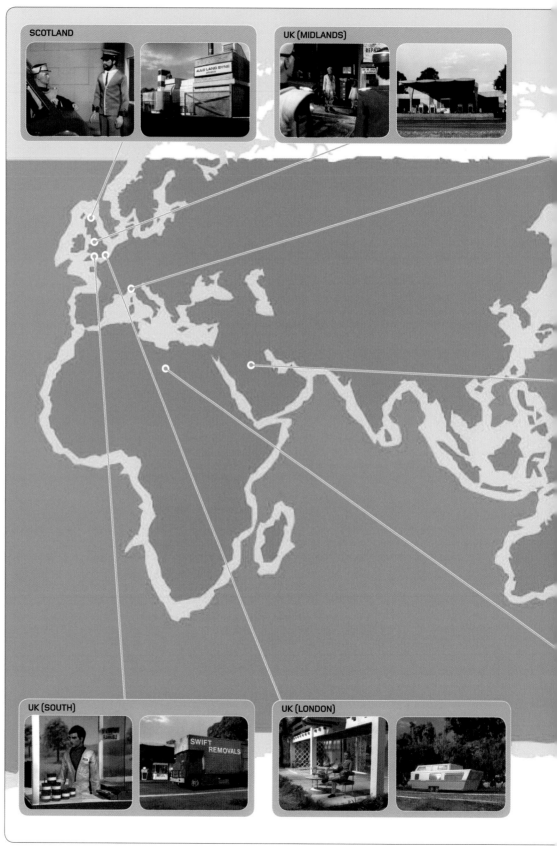

SCOTLAND

UK (MIDLANDS)

UK (SOUTH)

UK (LONDON)

Spectrum Pursuit Vehicles are stationed around the world in easily accessible locations. Each vehicle is maintained in full mission readiness by a local Spectrum agent and concealed in a carefully camouflaged storage unit. This map indicates a range of these stations and the local agents that operate them.

MONTE CARLO

NORTHERN CANADA

SAUDI ARABIA

NEW YORK CITY

SAHARA DESERT

NEVADA

SPECTRUM SALOON CAR

Spectrum Saloon Car
Technical data

LENGTH :	18ft
WIDTH :	8ft
WEIGHT :	1.5 tons
TOP SPEED :	200/250mph (depending on model)

PRIMARY DATAFILE

The Spectrum Saloon Car is a gas turbine powered five-seater vehicle which has been developed to provide a practical and comfortable means for Spectrum field agents to travel to incident zones by road. Maintained by Spectrum ground force units in the organisation's bases around the world, the cars are driven by local agents to any point where a field officer may require them. The saloon cars are also usually kept on standby at any airbase affiliated to Spectrum that the organisation might use to carry out a journey by Spectrum Passenger Jet.

Designed for ease of maintenance and internal engineering modification, the cars are regularly updated with improved components. Initially only capable of speeds approaching 200mph, upgraded turbines have now been fitted to some cars to enable them to reach greater speeds on super highways. The saloon car also incorporates many safety features, including an internal ribcage and roll bar to protect occupants should the car overturn, magnetic brakes, anti-puncture tyres, a stabilising fin for high speed cruising stability and instantaneous deceleration-activated airbags for driver and passengers.

The multiple uses to which the saloon cars are put range from incident zone patrols and road block management to local area investigations, convoy escort and emergency rapid response duties. The vehicle carries a variety of equipment, including traffic management barriers, high visibility clothing and emergency aid supplies.

SPECTRUM CODE NAME :
Captain Blue
OPERATIONAL DUTIES :
Field Agent
REAL NAME :
Adam Svenson
DATE OF BIRTH :
26 August 2035
PLACE OF BIRTH :
Boston, USA

BACKGROUND : A brilliant scholar and son of a wealthy New York financier. Won full scholarship to Harvard at age of 16. Attained first class honours in economics, technology, computer control, applied mathematics and aerodynamics. Seemed destined for business career, but joined World Aeronautic Society intending to become test pilot. Enthusiasm and fearless attitude as pilot led to transfer by superiors to security department with instructions to investigate and eliminate repeated security breaches. Succeeding against exceptional odds, his determination and tenacity attracted attention of Spectrum selection committee who offered him field agent post. Offer immediately accepted.

PERSONAL INTERESTS : Off-duty leisure pursuits include water-skiing, surfing and deep sea diving.

SPECTRUM SALOON CAR

The distinctive arrow-shaped saloon cars can reach speeds approaching 250mph in recently modified form due to its custom-built lightweight body shell and upgraded gas turbine power unit.

Spectrum Saloon Car

1. Transverse gearbox
2. Turbine combustion chamber
3. Compressor turbine
4. Power turbine
5. Exhaust filter and grille throws exhaust clear of other vehicles
6. Fuel tank
7. Rear storage compartment with access panels for turbine servicing
8. Emergency road adhesion braking system utilises quick-drying adhesive that is sprayed on to the tyres. This forms a second tread with road adhesion qualities. If the driver wishes to continue the journey, the second tread can be rapidly cut with an integral blade as the wheel rotates
9. Emergency braking liquid storage tank
10. Rear wheel suspension cantilever
11. Stabilising fin
12. Port side rear seating
13. Gas turbine ventilation duct
14. Air intake duct
15. Radio communications aerial
16. Cabin environment and entertainment controls
17. In-car radio and communications speaker
18. Steering wheel
19. Central computer maintaining engine and cabin environment via micro-sensors located throughout vehicle
20. Bullet-poof polarised windscreen
21. Compressed air tank inflates collision crash bags located under dashboard on both sides of the car
22. Interior air conditioning fans
23. Filtered air conditioning grille
24. Bullet-proof tyres
25. Magnetic brakes use opposing magnetic fields created by electromagnets controlled by the strength of the current supply activated by the brake pedal
26. Front emergency road-adhesion braking system
27. Air intake reduces tyre friction heat
28. Front wheel suspension linkage
29. Bevel and crown wheel drive to front axles
30. Oil cooler
31. Port driving mirror fairing
32. Twin-shaft six-speed gearbox
33. Laser projector and video camera linked to onboard TV monitor
34. Starboard infra-red scanner calculates and regulates distances between vehicles in conjunction with Highway Traffic Speed Control systems
35. Sidelights and direction indicators
36. Starboard headlight
37. Rapid-fire small arm; can be removed via underside panel and hand-held if necessary
38. Cahelium-strengthened hydraulic bolt; can be extended within the forward nose-cone chassis to ram suspected Mysteron vehicles. In normal driving conditions, the bolt remains retracted and the nose is designed to crumple in the event of an accidental collision with another vehicle

MAXIMUM SECURITY VEHICLE

The provision of secure transportation for the world's most important people was an integral aspect of Spectrum's original operational purpose. The Maximum Security Vehicle has been designed to meet this requirement in the most effective way possible.

Maximum Security Vehicle
Technical data

LENGTH:	24ft
WIDTH:	9ft
WEIGHT:	8 tons
TOP SPEED:	200mph

PRIMARY DATAFILE

Like the versatile Spectrum saloon car, the MSV was one of the few vehicles custom-built to meet Spectrum's specific needs. As road vehicles, however, they could not be more different. While the saloon car is fast and manoeuvrable, in comparison the Maximum Security Vehicle appears slow and cumbersome - the tortoise to the saloon car's hare. But like the tortoise, the MSV has a hard outer shell and a resilient inner strength.

Developed in association with the World Army Air Force, who offered all their experience in forms of ground combat to create the most 'attack-proof' vehicle conceivable, the Maximum Security Vehicle prototypes were subjected to rigorous bombardment and other forms of extreme military duress on the World Army's assault course before a final design was approved.

Hand-built to meticulous standards from the most durable materials known to man, the MSV offers the ultimate in comfort and security for its occupants. The utmost protection is provided by a quadruple-layer skin consisting of outer armour plating, a refrigeration honeycomb layer, a radiation damping membrane and an inner casing of cahelium-hardened steel.

Comfort comes in the form of deep padded seats, air conditioning and a refreshment cabinet. The inner compartments of the vehicle can be sealed completely and supplied with their own pressurised atmosphere for up to ten hours. Providing power for the MSV is a hybrid diesel electric system which can function concurrently or independently. This unit is supplied by fuel from giant tanks on each side of the vehicle and by long-duration solar collector batteries charged by external energy absorption strips running along the vehicle's central strengthening rib. Additional features include built-in radiation and toxic gas detectors and self-sealing missile-proof tyres.

SPECTRUM CODE NAME :
Captain Magenta
OPERATIONAL DUTIES :
Field Agent
REAL NAME :
Patrick Donaghue
DATE OF BIRTH :
17 May 2034
PLACE OF BIRTH :
Dublin, Ireland

BACKGROUND : Grew up in atmosphere of poverty and crime after family emigrated to New York in 2037. Encouraged to work hard and won scholarship to Yale University. Joined extremist Group 22 and jailed for part in anti-Bereznik riot. Graduated with degrees in physics, electrical engineering and technology, but bored by work as computer programmer turned to crime, organising efficient syndicate. Ambition and ingenuity resulted in his operating two-thirds of New York criminal organisations. Recruited by Spectrum on grounds of his inside knowledge of criminal world. Accepted following offer of World Government pardon.

PERSONAL INTERESTS : Designing fool-proof computerised security systems.

Maximum Security Vehicle

1. Power generator
2. Distributor box
3. Four of eight rotary diesel cylinders
4. Gearbox
5. Brake fluid cooler
6. Braking system cooling air duct
7. Brake fluid pressurisation cylinder
8. Pressurised hydraulic brake fluid cylinder
9. Drive shaft with universal joints
10. Bevel box
11. Armourglass viewport and anti-glare shutter
12. Shutter slot strengthening rib construction
13. Emergency water supply tank
14. Hull construction features armour plating, refrigeration and anti-radiation sandwich layer, and internal steel wall
15. Oxygen tanks built into vehicle doors operate when MSV is hermetically sealed
16. Oxygen pump
17. Air recycling unit using zyolithic crystals to siphon carbon dioxide from cabin
18. Food rations container accessed from passenger door interior
19. Fuel tanks
20. Driver's door
21. Fuel tank shut-off valve operated when emergency doors are opened
22. Two-seat passenger cabin
23. Passenger seat undersides fold open to access emergency personal hygiene, sanitation and waste-disposal equipment
24. Intercom, TV and external communications controls
25. Power-assisted door opening system
26. Cabin filtered-air vent: can be closed if MSV needs to be airtight
27. Air-vent directional nozzle
28. Port side passenger gull-wing door
29. Topside fin housing communications electronics
30. Access to driver's compartment is normally via passenger cabin, though in an emergency, twin forward-gull-wing hatches can be operated, though are normally sealed shut
31. Starboard driving seat
32. Fire extinguisher
33. Radiation detector
34. Armourglass anti-glare driver's view port
35. Anti-radiation lead window shutter: if in use, the MSV can be driven using TV cameras linked to instrument panel view screens

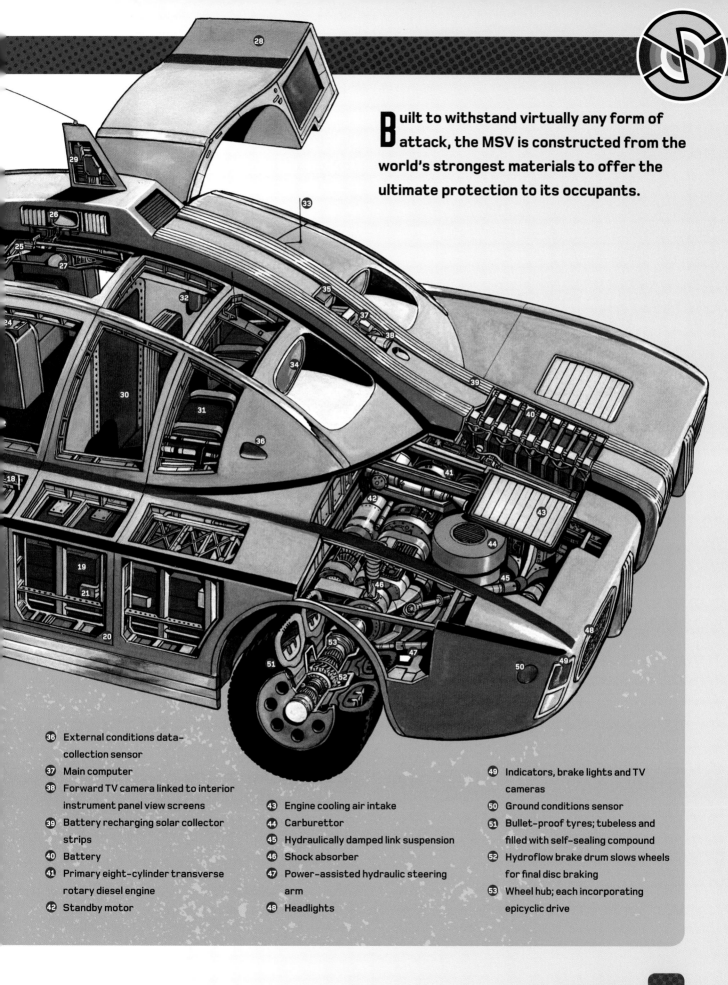

Built to withstand virtually any form of attack, the MSV is constructed from the world's strongest materials to offer the ultimate protection to its occupants.

36 External conditions data-collection sensor

37 Main computer

38 Forward TV camera linked to interior instrument panel view screens

39 Battery recharging solar collector strips

40 Battery

41 Primary eight-cylinder transverse rotary diesel engine

42 Standby motor

43 Engine cooling air intake

44 Carburettor

45 Hydraulically damped link suspension

46 Shock absorber

47 Power-assisted hydraulic steering arm

48 Headlights

49 Indicators, brake lights and TV cameras

50 Ground conditions sensor

51 Bullet-proof tyres; tubeless and filled with self-sealing compound

52 Hydroflow brake drum slows wheels for final disc braking

53 Wheel hub; each incorporating epicyclic drive

YELLOW FOX TRANSPORTER

If transportation of VIPs is required on a mission and Spectrum does not wish to draw attention to its presence it can call on the incongruous 'Yellow Fox' fleet of converted fuel tankers.

Yellow Fox Transporter
Technical data

LENGTH:	36ft
WIDTH:	9ft
WEIGHT:	5 tons
TOP SPEED:	110mph

PRIMARY DATAFILE

Developed by Spectrum's Covert Operations Agency as an ingenious solution to the problem posed by the frequent need to transport VIPs securely but in complete secrecy, the Yellow Fox is adapted from a conventional high octane fuel tanker. Originally designed by the Superon Fuel Corporation, now a division of Delta Petroleum, the tanker had already been purposefully engineered to carry a highly valuable commodity over long distances in a reliable and secure manner, leading its modification for Spectrum's purposes to involve little mechanical alteration.

For Spectrum's use, the main transverse diesel engine has been upgraded to provide more power, and is now supplemented by a heavy duty electric motor, while the suspension has been strengthened to support the reconstructed fuel pod. The driver's cabin has also been re-equipped with a computer-controlled engine management system and a compact communications console, in addition to being fitted with airtight doors and external vent seals coupled with compressed air tanks to create internal cabin pressurisation.

In contrast to the largely unaltered main body of the vehicle, the rear-mounted fuel pod has been entirely rebuilt with a cahelium-strengthened double-walled armoured skin to create a bomb-and-missile proof compartment for its passengers. Like the driver's cabin, the rear pod is also fitted with its own dedicated sealed environment pressurisation system, which can be immediately activated by external sensors. Entered by a combined rear step hatchway that can be hermetically sealed when closed, the passenger pod is fitted with a conference table and six swivel armchairs that can be turned towards a viewing monitor at the front of the compartment. This is linked to a communications control panel for video conferencing or the playback of filmed reports. Deeply padded wall panels offer impact protection in the event of attack or collision.

SPECTRUM CODE NAME :
Captain Ochre
OPERATIONAL DUTIES :
Field Agent
REAL NAME :
Richard Fraser
DATE OF BIRTH :
23 February 2035
PLACE OF BIRTH :
Detroit, USA

BACKGROUND : Learnt to fly at age 16 and left school at 18 aiming to enrol in World Army Air Force. Lack of sufficient qualifications led him to join World Government Police Corps. Character and ability emerged and after completing basic training became fascinated with detective work. Transferred to Chicago, his ingenuity and deductive abilities enabling him to infiltrate and overcome a major crime syndicate. Rapid promotion followed until officered position as supreme commander of WGPC. Decision to turn down post in favour of commanding his own division attracted attention of Spectrum and he was offered and accepted position of field agent.

PERSONAL INTERESTS : Retains his boyhood enthusiasm for flying and relaxes by building model aircraft.

Covert transportation for up to six passengers and a four- man crew is provided by the converted fuel tanker code-named 'Yellow Fox'.

Yellow Fox Transporter

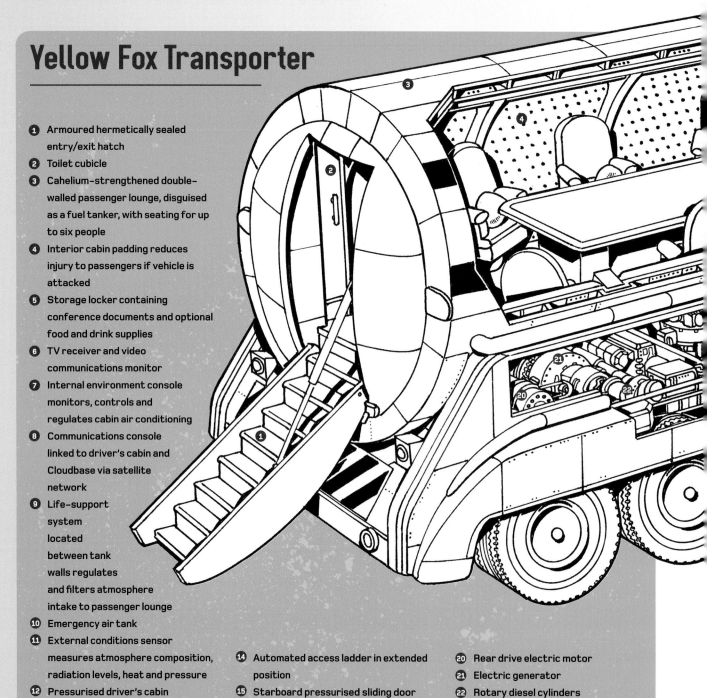

1. Armoured hermetically sealed entry/exit hatch
2. Toilet cubicle
3. Cahelium-strengthened double-walled passenger lounge, disguised as a fuel tanker, with seating for up to six people
4. Interior cabin padding reduces injury to passengers if vehicle is attacked
5. Storage locker containing conference documents and optional food and drink supplies
6. TV receiver and video communications monitor
7. Internal environment console monitors, controls and regulates cabin air conditioning
8. Communications console linked to driver's cabin and Cloudbase via satellite network
9. Life-support system located between tank walls regulates and filters atmosphere intake to passenger lounge
10. Emergency air tank
11. External conditions sensor measures atmosphere composition, radiation levels, heat and pressure
12. Pressurised driver's cabin
13. Starboard access ladder stowage bay, located under the floor, below the driver's seat; also duplicated on port side of vehicle
14. Automated access ladder in extended position
15. Starboard pressurised sliding door
16. Carburettor
17. Main transverse diesel engine
18. Gearbox
19. Starboard fuel tank
20. Rear drive electric motor
21. Electric generator
22. Rotary diesel cylinders
23. Hydraulic damped link suspension
24. Brake drum and power-assisted steering
25. Drive shaft

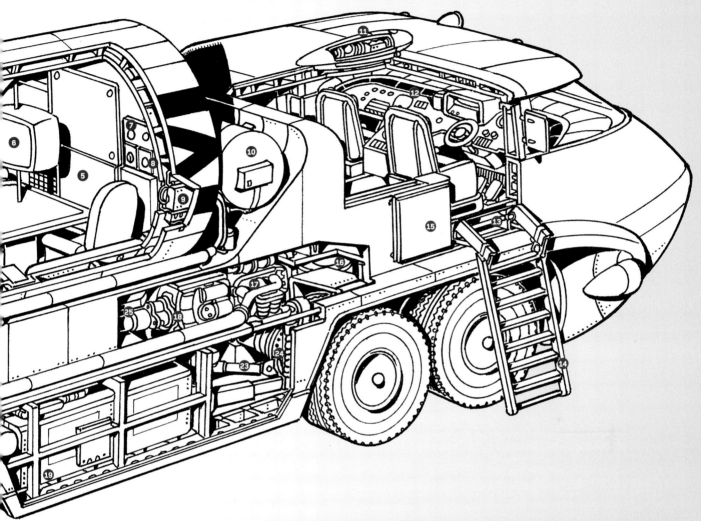

DETECTOR TRUCK

P rimarily intended to serve as a mobile communication and tracking vehicle, the Detector Trucks are also fitted with equipment capable of detecting sources of radiation.

Detector Truck
Technical data

LENGTH:	24ft
WIDTH:	9ft
WEIGHT:	3.5 tons
TOP SPEED:	120mph

PRIMARY DATAFILE

When originally conceived as a security organisation, one of Spectrum's primary duties would have been to detect and monitor possible threats posed by atomic devices or radioactive material, whether accidental or with malicious intent. Seeking a cost-effective means to do so, the Spectrum Logistics Agency devised the idea of refurbishing a newly superseded fleet of World Police public order control vehicles. Purposefully designed to assist in riot control and detect unlicensed pirate transmitters and receivers, the vehicles were practically perfect for Spectrum's purposes as purchased from the World Police decommissioned vehicles department.

Already fitted with a well tested, high frequency, multi-wavelength rotating bar antenna and recently upgraded communication equipment, the primary modification carried out by Spectrum was the installation of radiation detection systems, incorporating a long-range Geiger counter. Usually operated by a two-man crew in addition to a driver, the vehicle can be linked via satellite with other Detector Trucks in the vicinity to cross-coordinate signal sources detected by the scanner.

The satellite link also allows the Detector Truck to receive information beamed from the Spectrum Information Centre aboard Cloudbase and other electronic and radio wave transmission sources, in addition to supplying global positioning data to the navigation consoles in the driver's cabin. This enables the driver to select the most effective and direct route to an action zone and monitor information supplied by highway traffic control systems, local security services and other vehicles in the fleet.

Powered by forward-mounted fuel cells, the Detector Truck is also fitted with a reinforced external crash bar and signal interference shielding.

SPECTRUM CODE NAME :
Captain Grey
OPERATIONAL DUTIES :
Field Agent
REAL NAME :
Bradley Holden
DATE OF BIRTH :
4 March 2033
PLACE OF BIRTH :
Chicago, USA

BACKGROUND : Educated at World Navy San Diego academy where he gained degrees in navigation, aqua-technology and computer control. Immediately enrolled in World Navy submarine service on graduating. Trained as officer and given command of World Navy submarine. Showing brilliant tactics, cool reaction to pressure and tremendous valour on duty, quick thinking and alertness also saved crew and submarine from falling into enemy hands. With formation of World Aquanaut Security Patrol transferred and promoted to security commander. During testing of prototype submarine later designated 'Stingray', took part in daring campaigns comparable to his successor's. Possessing all the qualifications needed by Spectrum, his reputation led him to be recruited as field agent.

PERSONAL INTERESTS : Developing new swimming techniques and miniaturised diving equipment.

DETECTOR TRUCK

In the event of a radiation leak or for tracking coordination purposes, Detector Truck fleets can be mobilised from Spectrum bases in major cities to carry out effective monitoring.

Detector Truck overview

1. Reinforced crash bar
2. Air inlet for filtered engine and fuel-cell cooling systems
3. Navigator's console uses information from the monitoring bay's systems and Cloudbase to select the most direct or efficient route to the action zone. Data is also supplied by highway traffic control systems, other vehicles in the fleet or security services
4. Battery
5. Multi-unit fuel-cell-fed electricity generator, powered by air, oxygen and hydrogen stored in adjacent tanks above cab
6. Port side electric motor, powered by the adjacent fuel-cell-fed generator above

7. Steering console, with power-assisted steering, engine monitoring and video communications unit
8. Steering arm and drive. This passes through the gearbox and bevel drive to serve the front and rear wheels
9. Magnetic brake drum
10. Hydrogen fuel cells

11. Antenna motor and cooling systems control console
12. Waveform monitor
13. Sync monitor
14. Port entry hatch
15. Monitoring bay

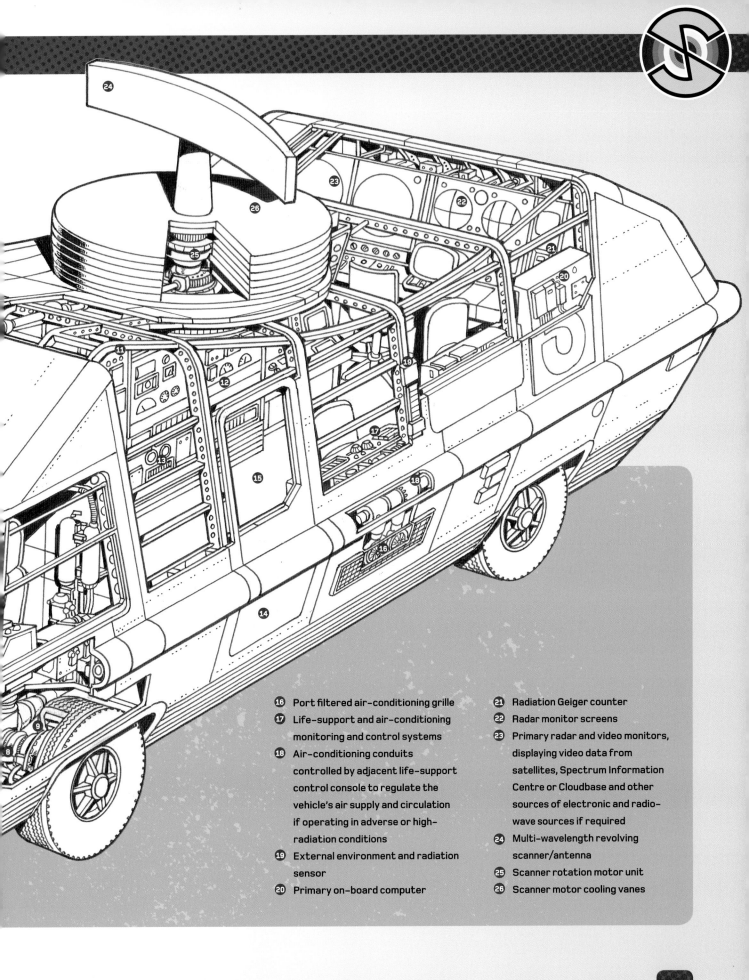

16 Port filtered air-conditioning grille

17 Life-support and air-conditioning monitoring and control systems

18 Air-conditioning conduits controlled by adjacent life-support control console to regulate the vehicle's air supply and circulation if operating in adverse or high-radiation conditions

19 External environment and radiation sensor

20 Primary on-board computer

21 Radiation Geiger counter

22 Radar monitor screens

23 Primary radar and video monitors, displaying video data from satellites, Spectrum Information Centre or Cloudbase and other sources of electronic and radio-wave sources if required

24 Multi-wavelength revolving scanner/antenna

25 Scanner rotation motor unit

26 Scanner motor cooling vanes

SPECTRUM HOVERCRAFT

In coastal zones or areas of rough and inhospitable terrain, Spectrum hovercraft provide a fast and efficient means of transportation.

Hovercraft
Technical data

LENGTH:	50ft
WIDTH:	23ft
WEIGHT:	4.5 tons
TOP SPEED:	100mph

PRIMARY DATAFILE

Developed in the Sydney all-terrain vehicle workshops of Universal Engineering Incorporated, the Spectrum hovercraft was initially designed for use by the World Army Air Force. Demands for a larger and more adaptable vehicle led the service to turn down the concept, but Spectrum's chief design officer Captain Viridian, impressed by the results of UEI's work, saw it as a perfect addition to Spectrum's worldwide fleet of patrol vehicles.

The craft utilises conventional hovercraft technology, but is powered by a newly developed Neutomic Generator power system which when kept under correct operating temperature maintains it in flight for repeated journeys without the need for reprocessing. Forward thrust is provided by twin compressor turbines mounted beneath the tailplane, which also serves as the craft's rudder. The turbines provide enough thrust to propel the craft at speeds in excess of 100mph.

Ideal for use in coastal and desert areas, the Amazonian rainforests or the Louisiana bayou, the hovercraft can carry two passengers in addition to its two-man crew. A rear cabin is equipped with basic facilities and a range of tools and protective clothing, and in the case of craft serving more remote parts of the world, supplies are stored on board to allow for trips lasting several days to be made, in addition to the equipment required to set up a temporary base camp.

In common with other Spectrum vehicles that require specialised skill to operate safely and efficiently, a dedicated training base has been set up connected to a conveniently located Spectrum Academy. Largely due to its proximity to Universal Engineering's existing outback testing ground and the rugged surrounding terrain, Spectrum's Base Koala was deemed ideal to be designated as the hovercraft training centre.

SPECTRUM CADETS

The recruitment of suitable officers and ancillary operatives to maintain Spectrum's pre-eminence as the world's leading security service remains a constant challenge. To ensure this need is met with the best possible individuals available, Spectrum recruitment officers permanently monitor the intake of other World Government services, and regularly offer positions to the most able and experienced men and women already serving. In addition, Spectrum also recruits likely candidates directly from international military training schools to enrol as cadets, with particular emphasis on those who exhibit wide-ranging abilities.

All newly recruited members of Spectrum, whatever their level of experience, are then put through rigorous instruction courses at Spectrum's four training academies around the world. These are Base Eagle, attached to the World Army Air Force base at Boscombe Down, which specialises in all forms of flight training and multi-terrain driving skills, Base Dolphin in Indonesia, which focuses on aquatic expertise, Base White Owl in Washington State where the emphasis is on intelligence development, and Base Koala in Australia which instructs students in hovercraft operation and survival skills.

Once recruits have passed through the required programmes at all four bases, they are then considered eligible to become fully endorsed permanent members of Spectrum.

SPECTRUM HOVERCRAFT

Spectrum hovercraft

1. Forward ground conditions sensor
2. Control cabin: Forward seats and consoles for pilot and co-pilot, rear seats for passengers and/or observers
3. Instrument nacelle reading windspeed and external temperature, with integrated radar system
4. Rear compartment incorporates port and starboard exit doors, eating facilities and supplies for longer journeys
5. Toilet
6. Port access hatch
7. Communications antenna
8. Dual rotors drive air downwards towards air-cushion outlets
9. Dual rotor bearings
10. Bevel box and drive serving rotor
11. Rotor safety grille prevents debris or wildlife damaging the rotor blade
12. Gearbox

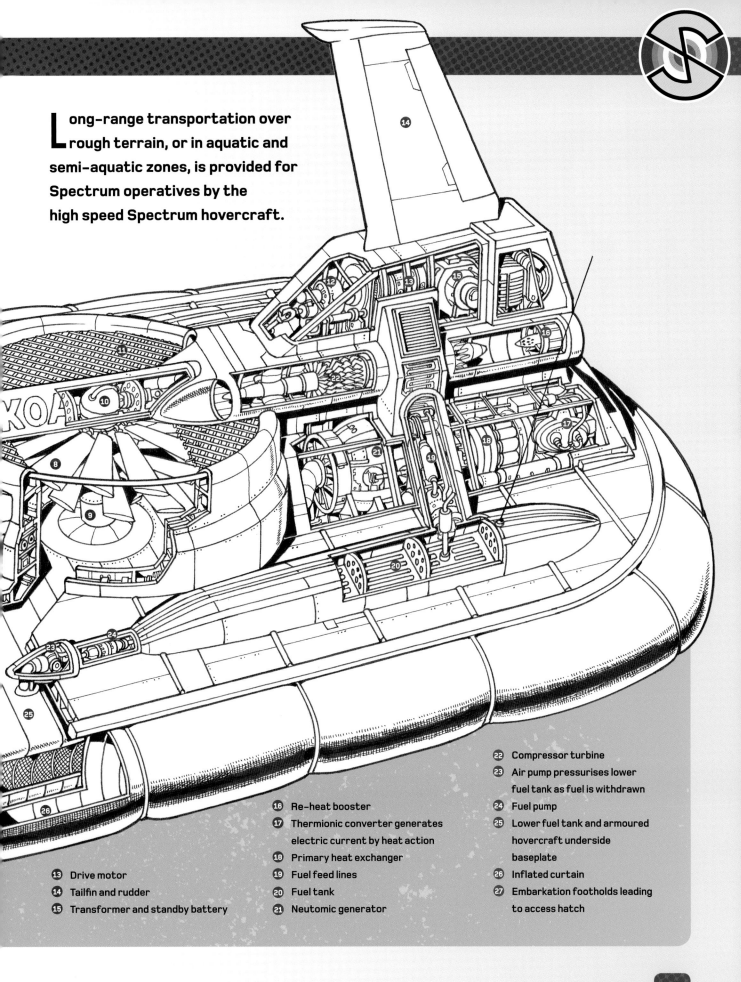

Long-range transportation over rough terrain, or in aquatic and semi-aquatic zones, is provided for Spectrum operatives by the high speed Spectrum hovercraft.

13 Drive motor
14 Tailfin and rudder
15 Transformer and standby battery

16 Re-heat booster
17 Thermionic converter generates electric current by heat action
18 Primary heat exchanger
19 Fuel feed lines
20 Fuel tank
21 Neutomic generator

22 Compressor turbine
23 Air pump pressurises lower fuel tank as fuel is withdrawn
24 Fuel pump
25 Lower fuel tank and armoured hovercraft underside baseplate
26 Inflated curtain
27 Embarkation footholds leading to access hatch

ANGEL LAUNCH SYSTEM

Designed to take full advantage of the decision to base Spectrum's headquarters aboard an airborne carrier, the Angel launch system enables a flight of aircraft to be launched in record time.

Launch Sequence

Once the command to launch all Angels has been given, Angel One takes off immediately **1**, while Lt Green notifies the duty Angels via their epaulettes **2** to take up position in their seats **3**. These are transported from the Amber Room to a clear pressurised casing beneath their aircraft **4** and elevated into the craft **5** prior to launch **6**.

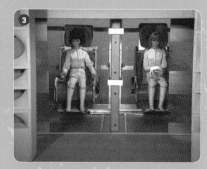

SPECTRUM CODE NAME :

Destiny Angel

OPERATIONAL DUTIES :

Angel Flight Pilot

REAL NAME :

Juliette Pontoin

DATE OF BIRTH :

23 August 2040

PLACE OF BIRTH :

Paris, France

PRIMARY DATAFILE

One of the most ingeniously conceived features of Cloudbase, the Angel Interceptor catapult launch and air crew access system has been expertly designed and engineered for maximum crew comfort and functional reliability. Situated on the opposite side of Cloudbase to the command centre, the Angel flight's dedicated runway runs almost the entire length of the main body with its three catapult launchers positioned directly above the Amber Room, a circular structure which serves as the Angel pilots' standby lounge.

Tastefully decorated in pastel colours to create a relaxing atmosphere, the Amber Room incorporates a library of books, films and records, in addition to storage units containing a variety of games and pastimes to ensure the Angels can enjoy their time spent off-duty or on standby. Working a rotating schedule of four-hour duty shifts, one Angel is always stationed in Angel One awaiting instructions to launch, while two others are ready at a moment's notice to be transported aloft to their machines via the injector seat conveyor system. This is accessed through frosted sliding doors behind which seats for Angels Two and Three are located.

Having taken up position in their seats the two Angels are elevated to the pressurised deck above the Amber Room, rotated through 90 degrees and transversely transported into position beneath their aircraft. Then mounted on the cockpit underside section, the occupied flying seat is hydraulically lifted into position through a sealed transparent conveyor casing which is retracted once the entire cockpit unit is securely clamped into position. The aircraft is then ready to launch.

On returning from duty, the reverse procedure is carried out once the aircraft is back in place on the flight deck. This is achieved by means of an elevating ramp section provided for each aircraft. Precision skill is required by each pilot to manoeuvre their craft into position above the ramp's magnetic guidance tracks from which it can be automatically returned to its launch station once the ramp has retracted.

BACKGROUND : Daughter of a Parisian textile manufacturer. Educated at convent school and Rome University. After taking degrees in telecommunications and weather control, joined World Army Air Force where she was assigned to Intelligence Corps. Taught to fly as part of basic training, she soon became known for skill as pilot and intelligence officer. Promoted to commander of Women's Fighter Squadron where she excelled in aerial combat tactics. After three years in the force decided to resign post and form firm of flying contractors. Track record with WAAF resulted in her being approached by Spectrum selection committee. Challenge offered led her to accept position of Angel pilot.

PERSONAL INTERESTS : Inspired by family background in textiles and fashion, enjoys designing and tailoring own clothes.

ANGEL LAUNCH SYSTEM

Stationed on a dedicated flight deck fitted with a catapult launch system, three Angel aircraft can be accessed directly by their pilots from the Amber Room standby lounge situated beneath the aircrafts' launch positions.

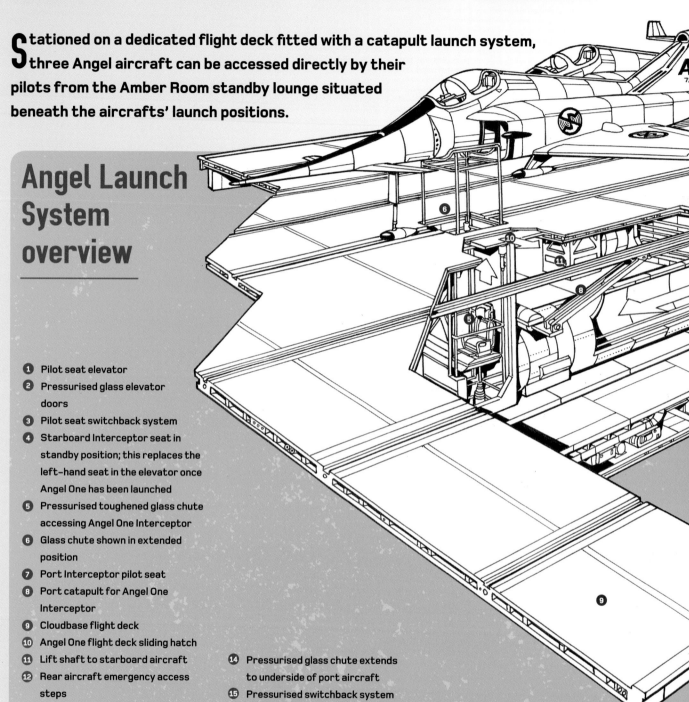

Angel Launch System overview

1. Pilot seat elevator
2. Pressurised glass elevator doors
3. Pilot seat switchback system
4. Starboard Interceptor seat in standby position; this replaces the left-hand seat in the elevator once Angel One has been launched
5. Pressurised toughened glass chute accessing Angel One Interceptor
6. Glass chute shown in extended position
7. Port Interceptor pilot seat
8. Port catapult for Angel One Interceptor
9. Cloudbase flight deck
10. Angel One flight deck sliding hatch
11. Lift shaft to starboard aircraft
12. Rear aircraft emergency access steps
13. Angel Interceptor underside cockpit pressure hatch: this retracts when the glass chute clamps into position and the pilot is raised into the cockpit. The underside of the aircraft located at the bottom of the lift shaft and chute provides a double seal
14. Pressurised glass chute extends to underside of port aircraft
15. Pressurised switchback system accessing port aircraft
16. Lift shaft incorporating toughened pressurised glass chute. With the pilot and seat in place, the chute is raised to the underside of the Interceptor
17. Port aircraft emergency access passage
18. The Amber Room: standby lounge for the Angel pilots
19. Lift doors to rest of Cloudbase
20. Emergency steps leading to access passage in case of power failure
21. Ventilation and heating systems

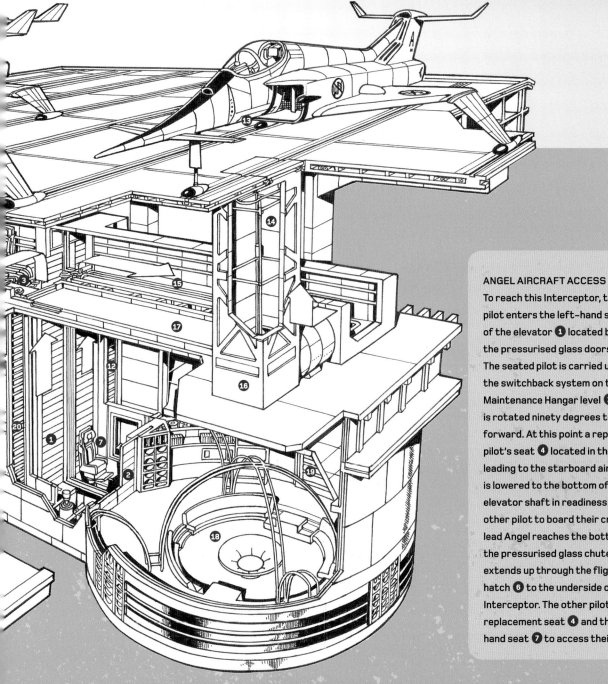

ANGEL AIRCRAFT ACCESS

To reach this Interceptor, the pilot enters the left-hand side of the elevator ❶ located behind the pressurised glass doors ❷. The seated pilot is carried up to the switchback system on the Maintenance Hangar level ❸ and is rotated ninety degrees to face forward. At this point a replacement pilot's seat ❹ located in the shaft leading to the starboard aircraft, is lowered to the bottom of the elevator shaft in readiness for the other pilot to board their craft. The lead Angel reaches the bottom of the pressurised glass chute ❺ which extends up through the flight deck hatch ❻ to the underside of the Interceptor. The other pilots use the replacement seat ❹ and the right-hand seat ❼ to access their aircraft.

ANGEL LANDING SEQUENCE

Landing ramp at rear of Angel flight deck is raised ❶ to allow Angel aircraft to land using vertical jets ❷. Angel aircraft is clamped to launch deck for relaunch.

ANGEL INTERCEPTOR

Spectrum's single-seater Angel Interceptor is the most advanced fighter aircraft in the world. Capable of speeds beyond Mach 3, a squadron stands ready aboard Cloudbase at all times.

Angel Interceptor
Technical data

LENGTH :	60ft
WINGSPAN :	35ft
WEIGHT :	40,100lbs
TOP SPEED :	3,000+ mph (currently under review)
RANGE :	4,500 miles

PRIMARY DATAFILE

When the creation of Spectrum was first proposed, agreement was quickly reached that the organisation would operate more efficiently by being able to command its own squadron of fighter aircraft. An equally unanimous decision confirmed that the ideal aircraft to fulfil Spectrum's needs was the World Army Air Force's newly commissioned Viper fighter built by International Engineering at their Fairfield factory near Farnborough in England. Capable of reaching speeds approaching Mach 3, and possessing high manoeuvrability, no other fighter aircraft in production could match its capabilities.

The potential to improve the Viper's existing capabilities was also noted, and Spectrum's Research and Development Agency ordered a nut and bolt overhaul of the machine to enhance its already superlative speed and performance. Once it had been decided that the aircraft would be launched from an airborne carrier, modifications were also introduced to increase its operating height and adapt the airframe beneath the cockpit to allow the section under the pilot's seat to be elevated into position through a sealed pressurised tube.

The aircraft's weaponry was also upgraded to incorporate a cannon capable of firing a variety of ammunition, including tracer and armour-piercing bullets in addition to rocket shells, with further batteries of air to air and air to ground missiles positioned at each side. After extensive testing it was found that the power of the twin turbojets could be increased through the newly developed Coboltibe enhancement process introduced by Spectrum's Bensheba refinery. This boosted thrust produced by the craft's ramjet to enable speeds in excess of Mach 3, and potentially up to Mach 4, to be achieved.

The newly renamed Angel Interceptor's most revolutionary new modifications however were to the aircraft's control systems. New hyper-responsive units were installed and these proved particularly suitable for use by female pilots, who were found to possess the psychologically tested qualities needed to optimise their operational potential. For this reason the Angel aircraft's crew was recruited from the ranks of experienced female pilots.

In common with other Spectrum craft, the Angel Interceptor is constantly being upgraded, with the latest addition to its strike capabilities being a newly developed electrode ray cannon capable of destroying Mysteronised ground and air targets at long range.

SPECTRUM CODE NAME :
Rhapsody Angel
OPERATIONAL DUTIES :
Angel Flight Pilot
REAL NAME :
Diane Simms
DATE OF BIRTH :
27 April 2043
PLACE OF BIRTH :
London, England

BACKGROUND : Public school educated daughter of World Government official Lord Robert Simms. Studied at London University, gaining degrees in law and sociology. Chance meeting with head of Federal Agents Bureau Lady Penelope Creighton-Ward at dull debutantes party led to offer of special training with organisation. After initial training completed with special commendation for flying skills, joined bureau as agent. Succeeded in carrying out many perilous missions against enemy spy rings. Took over supreme command of bureau when Creighton-Ward departed for unspecified reasons, rumoured to involve joining a newly formed secret rescue organisation. Intelligence and coolness in face of danger led her to become most sought-after agent in Europe. When FAB closed down following formation of USS, joined Euro-charter airline as chief security officer prior to recruitment by Spectrum.

PERSONAL INTERESTS : Enjoys games involving intellectual skill – particularly chess.

ANGEL INTERCEPTOR

Spectrum's delta wing fighter aircraft is adapted from the proven World Army Air Force Viper, its extensive modifications providing the organisation with unsurpassed long-range strike capability.

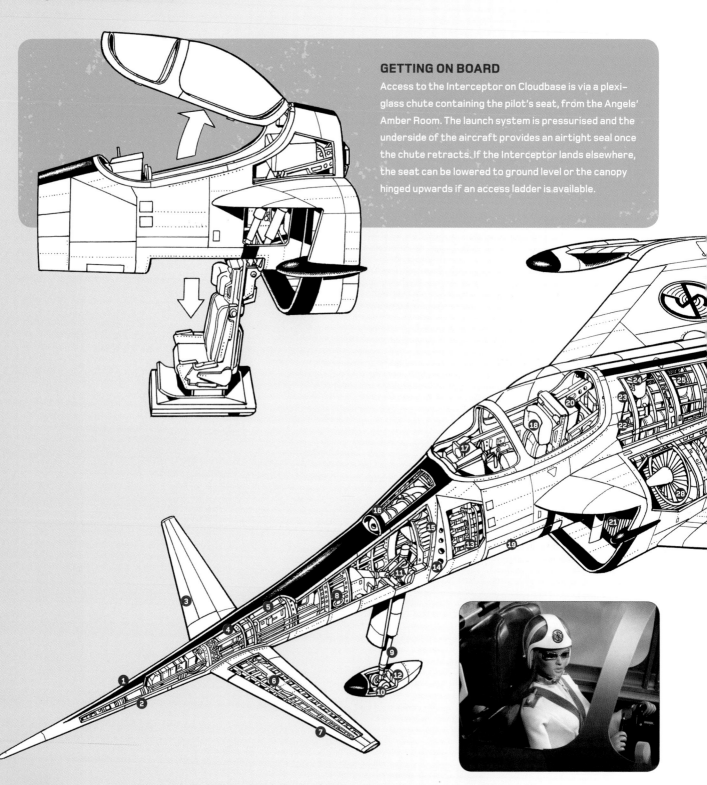

GETTING ON BOARD

Access to the Interceptor on Cloudbase is via a plexi-glass chute containing the pilot's seat, from the Angels' Amber Room. The launch system is pressurised and the underside of the aircraft provides an airtight seal once the chute retracts. If the Interceptor lands elsewhere, the seat can be lowered to ground level or the canopy hinged upwards if an access ladder is available.

Angel Interceptor

1. Anti-glare aircraft nose stripe
2. Radar scanner
3. Forward starboard stabiliser
4. External air pressure and temperature recorder
5. Wind-speed recorder
6. Forward port stabiliser multi-spar mounting rib
7. Forward stabilisers provide stabilising at high speed and prevent nose dip when full throttle is applied suddenly
8. Radar signal digital decoder
9. Telescopic shock-absorbing strut
10. Retracted landing wheels
11. Torque scissor links
12. Cloudbase launch system electromagnet
13. Port air-to-air and air-to-ground missiles
14. Missile launch tubes
15. Ammunition feed chute
16. Main cannon: fires a range of rocket, shell, armour-piercing and tracer ammunition
17. Instrument panel shroud and gunsight
18. Ejection seat
19. Underside pilot's entry/exit hatch
20. Flight computer
21. Port air intake
22. Cabin pressure regulator
23. Radio and electronics bay
24. Satellite communications antenna
25. Cabin pressurisation nitrogen cylinder
26. Main inboard fuel tank
27. VTOL thruster
28. Compressor intake fan
29. Port engine multi-stage compressors
30. Combustion chamber
31. Heat exchanger
32. Hydraulic reservoir
33. Lower tail re-heat air vents
34. Re-heat ring
35. Variable-mode afterburner
36. Bled air duct from turbine used for deflector braking
37. Emergency braking retro-rocket
38. Port wing brace
39. Aileron and leading-edge servo valves
40. Port wing fuel tanks
41. Leading-edge flap
42. Multi-spar mounting rib
43. Port aileron
44. Aileron power control jacks
45. Cahelium-strengthened port wing-tip mounting stanchion
46. Wing-tip spar mounting rib
47. Electro-magnets in landing gear allow aircraft to take off along Cloudbase's flight deck grooves, and also assist in landing when the flap at the end of the runway is used
48. Port wing wheels: usually retracted, but used if aircraft needs to take off or land from runway other than Cloudbase

SPECTRUM PASSENGER JET

Spectrum operatives' primary means of transport between Cloudbase and the ground, the streamlined passenger jets can reach mission zones at supersonic speed.

Spectrum Passenger Jet
Technical data

LENGTH :	78ft
WINGSPAN :	37ft
WEIGHT :	630,427lbs
TOP SPEED :	1,125mph
RANGE :	12,000 miles

PRIMARY DATAFILE

Providing fast and efficient transport for Spectrum's field officers and VIPs to and from Cloudbase, a fleet of Spectrum Passenger Jets operates from Spectrum-affiliated World Government service airbases around the world. Originally designed by Universal Aero to offer high altitude supersonic transportation for civilian and business users under the project name 'TVR 4', the mounting cost of development resulted in the aircraft not proving commercially viable. Realising it was perfect for their purposes, Spectrum agreed to purchase the patent and have it put into production for the organisation's sole use.

Powered by twin turbo jets modified by Spectrum's engineers to boost speed and endurance, the SPJ has an operating range of 12,000 miles. To increase manoeuvrability and stability in flight, rotating wing sections operated by a high tensile activated rod can be positioned with the aid of computer-monitored sensors. This revolutionary technology can also be utilised as an air-brake when landing on short runways, and its incorporation in the design sealed Spectrum's decision to acquire sole rights to the aircraft once the plan to locate its headquarters aboard an airborne carrier had been approved, due to the inherently short length of the carrier's runway.

Another ingenious aspect of the passenger jet's design is the modular pod unit construction of the passenger cabin. This allows alternative 'pods' to be substituted in place of the standard seven-passenger compartment at short notice to convert the aircraft to a personnel carrier or to provide it with conference facilities.

Since entering service with Spectrum, very few modifications have been made, although following the manifestation of the Mysteron threat, the non-combat status of the aircraft has been revised with the incorporation of a cannon unit similar to that installed in the Angel Interceptors. Further radical modifications are also on Captain Viridian's drawing board which include a redesigned wing profile and additional engines to increase range and speed.

SPECTRUM CODE NAME :
Melody Angel
OPERATIONAL DUTIES :
Angel Flight Pilot
REAL NAME :
Magnolia Jones
DATE OF BIRTH :
10 January 2043
PLACE OF BIRTH :
Atlanta, USA

BACKGROUND : Grew up with four brothers. Became involved with motor racing at an early age. Leaving school at 15 with no qualifications, she became a professional racing driver. Agreed to attend Swiss finishing school at wish of parents after learning she could take flying lessons. Discovering passion for flying, she joined World Army Air Force after being expelled from finishing school for unruly behaviour. After entering service, trained as test pilot and recognition of her skill led to her being assigned to fly experimental XKF 115. Feared dead after contact lost with aircraft over South Seas, but returned after building own craft from wreckage. Recruited by Spectrum after leaving WAAF to become freelance pilot.

PERSONAL INTERESTS : Keen on learning foreign languages. Is currently being taught Japanese by Harmony Angel.

SPECTRUM PASSENGER JET

Capable of transporting two crew and seven passengers in its standard form, the supersonic SPJ incorporates radical design features enabling to operate from short runways.

Spectrum Passenger Jet

1. Nose probe with air speed, gust detectors and pressure instrumentation
2. Radar scanner dish
3. Radar mounting and tracking mechanism
4. International Engineering Rosenthal Mk9 multi-mode radar scanner
5. Avionics equipment bay
6. Pilot's instrument console
7. Nose wheel doors
8. Aft-retracting nose wheel
9. Nose wheel stowage well
10. Communications aerials
11. Port stabiliser maintains stability at supersonic speeds and ensures a nose-up attitude when landing
12. Fuel tanks incorporated into fuselage construction
13. Fuel feed lines
14. Passenger cabin can be configured for a variety of purposes: a VIP lounge, conference or planning room, or with full-capacity seating as a personnel carrier

15. Passenger cabin inner door
16. Passenger entry/exit vestibule
17. Port entry inner door
18. Extended entry ladder
19. Starboard toilet and washroom on other side of central linking passage
20. Port toilet and washroom
21. Food preparation area
22. Food storage area
23. Port undercarriage stowage doors
24. Port rear undercarriage
25. Undercarriage retraction hydraulics

26. Wheel retraction pivot: wheels fold under dual struts before retracting up into undercarriage stowage well in fuselage
27. Wing position hydraulic rams
28. Wing movement bracket and control box
29. Compressor
30. Heat exchanger
31. Turbine, driving compressor
32. Bleed-off air duct for retro braking
33. Passive tail warning radar unit
34. Tailfin lower rudder

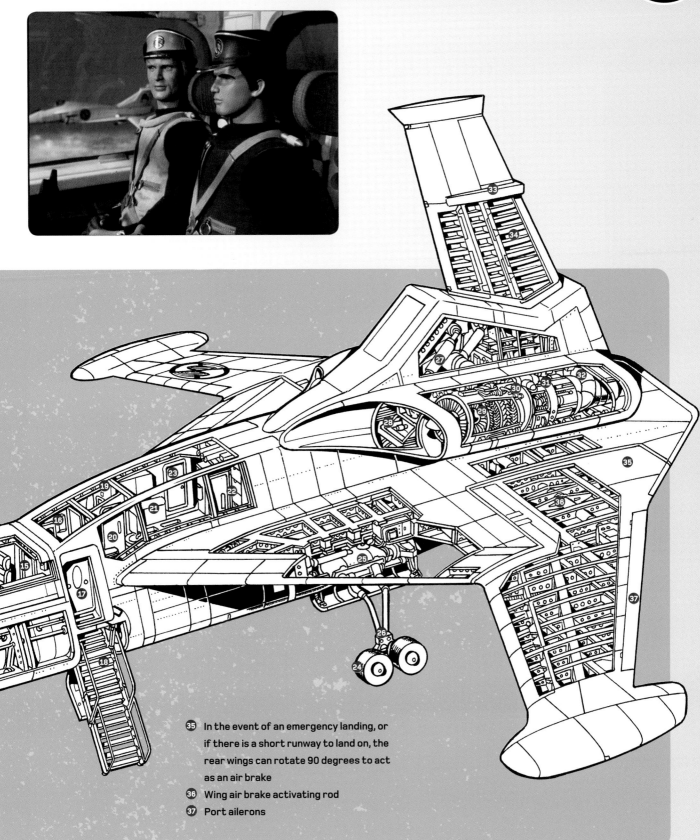

35 In the event of an emergency landing, or if there is a short runway to land on, the rear wings can rotate 90 degrees to act as an air brake

36 Wing air brake activating rod

37 Port ailerons

SPECTRUM HELICOPTER

Stationed at ground bases around the world, Spectrum Helicopters allow field agents to travel to any area otherwise inaccessible by other means of transport.

Spectrum Helicopter
Technical data

LENGTH :	45ft
WIDTH :	21ft
WEIGHT :	37,500lbs
TOP SPEED :	302mph
RANGE :	300 miles

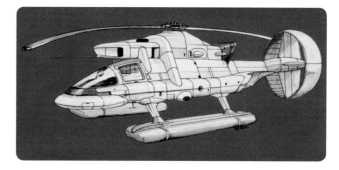

PRIMARY DATAFILE

Like the Spectrum Passenger jet, the Spectrum Helicopter is derived from an existing design, in this case Universal Engineering's tried and tested Rotar helicopter, which has served successfully with the World Army Air Force for a number of years. As the original design perfectly served Spectrum's purposes by providing a short-range means of aerial transport suitable for operating in areas of rough or unstable terrain, or at sea, very few modifications have been made, one of the few being to convert the engines to run with fuel synthesised at Spectrum's Bensheba refinery using the Harrison process. This enhances fuel economy, enabling the vehicle to stay airborne for a round trip of 300 miles or 24 hours of local patrol and escort duties.

Built around a tubular and box section frame, fitted with simple and reliable mechanical components, the helicopter is particularly robust and easy to maintain. The streamlined cabin and engine housing are ergonomically designed to offer little wind resistance, and additional speed is available through the use of booster jets. As an extra safety feature the directional vanes on the rear ring tail unit, combined with the vehicle's complex air surfaces, allow it to glide to the ground in the event of main engine failure.

Apart from providing structural integrity, the tubular upper part of the helicopter's frame also circulates air from the gearbox cooling intake to the cabin heating unit, the de-icing system and the landing float air-bag compressor. This enables the Maylon-bonded outer skin to be inflated to the most suitable pressure required for specific landing surfaces.

Capable of flying at speeds at over 300mph, the helicopter can carry four passengers in addition to the pilot. A rear cabin compartment contains communications electronics, storage units for field equipment and a stretcher unit for use by injured operatives which can be lowered from the underside of the craft. The rear compartment also houses the computer processor for the helicopter's Omni-scanner, a screen displaying a computer generated image of the local terrain incorporating the positions of any active Spectrum operatives.

SPECTRUM CODE NAME :
Harmony Angel
OPERATIONAL DUTIES :
Angel Flight Pilot
REAL NAME :
Chan Kwan
DATE OF BIRTH :
19 June 2042
PLACE OF BIRTH :
Tokyo, Japan

BACKGROUND : Daughter of wealthy flying taxi firm owner. Grew up in world of high speed jets. Educated at Tokyo High School and finishing school in London. Studied physics and aerodynamics at Tokyo University. Maintained interest in flying by becoming member of Tokyo flying club. After graduation spent two years perfecting flying skills prior to embarking on single- handed round-the-world flight. After abandoning first attempt in order to rescue crew of fire-stricken tanker, made successful record-breaking attempt six months later. On death of father became head of his Peking flying taxi business, expanding it into world's largest. Dedication and flying skill led to her recruitment by Spectrum.

PERSONAL INTERESTS : Enjoys sport and martial arts. Currently training fellow pilots in judo and karate.

SPECTRUM HELICOPTER

O ne of Spectrum's most useful general purpose vehicles, the helicopter can fly at speeds in the region of 300mph and is regularly used for escort, patrol or observation duties.

Spectrum Helicopter

1. Tailplane rudder
2. Tailplane rudder actuators
3. Booster rocket fuel tanks
4. Emergency rocket booster
5. Booster turbojet for attaining maximum speed in forward flight
6. Fuel tanks
7. Bleed–off ducts pass hot air through turbojet support member to lower exhaust port. The air is also bled off to a compressor which inflates the landing floats
8. Oil cooling system
9. Gearbox
10. Rotor head
11. Gearbox cooling intake
12. Turbojet support member
13. Starboard turbojet driving rotor via gearbox
14. Access door to electronics and storage bay, and underside entry hatch
15. Starboard emergency exit hatch
16. Starboard air intake
17. Bled–air duct serving float-inflation system
18. Starboard landing float: designed to land on any surface including water, these can be inflated to any required pressure according to the terrain conditions. Air is contained within an inner tube inside a Maylon-bonded outer skin
19. Airflow regulator valves
20. Inner air tube cradle supports
21. Cooling air exhaust outlet
22. Retracted access ladder
23. Underside entry hatch
24. Equipment stowage
25. Control console
26. Pilot's seat
27. Avionics shroud and autopilot
28. Variable–mode gun attachment: a variety of small armaments can be fitted, including a rocket launcher or machine gun
29. Flight instruments measuring wind speed, air pressure and temperature
30. Wide–angle dual-dish radar system
31. External environment sensor

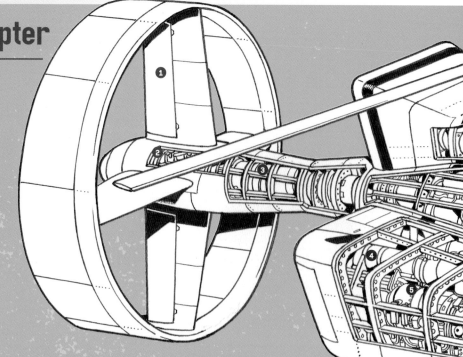

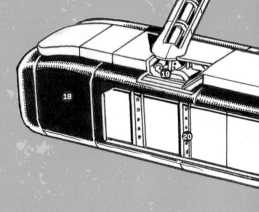

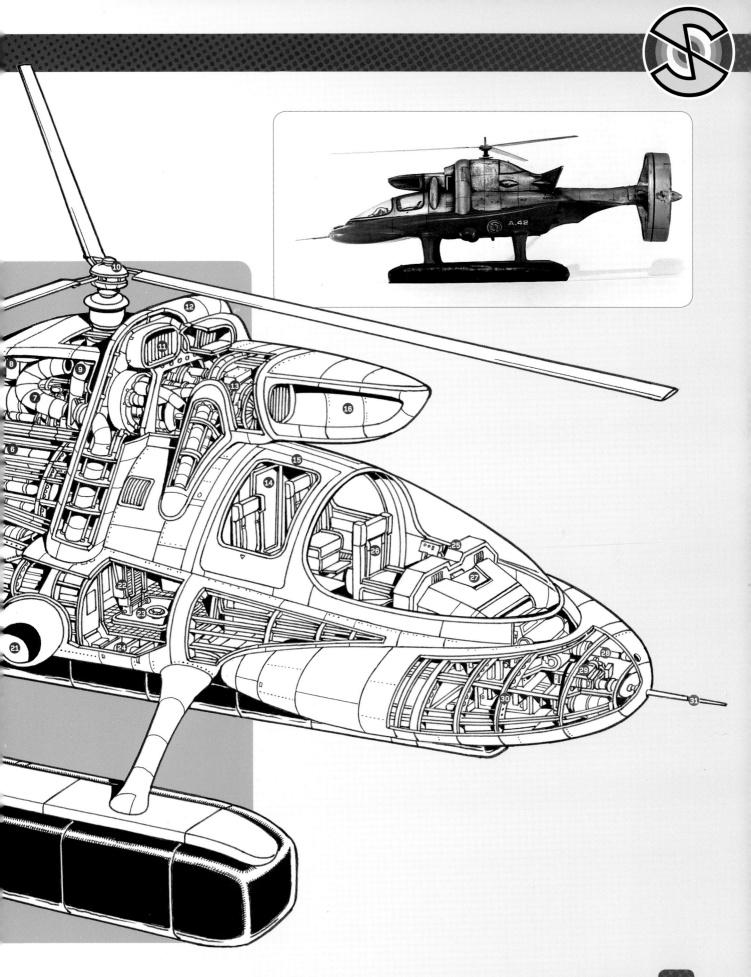

MAGNACOPTER

O ften used by Spectrum to transport groups of military and World Government officials on long-distance flights, the Magnacopter can also be used as a mobile conference and command centre.

Magnacopter
Technical data

LENGTH:	200ft
WIDTH:	60ft
WEIGHT:	117,180lbs
TOP SPEED:	290mph
RANGE:	12,000 miles

PRIMARY DATAFILE

One of the oldest vehicles that Spectrum regularly makes use of in the course of its operational duties, the Magnacopter first entered service with the World Army Air Force in the mid-2050s. Originally designed for use as a troop carrier to enable the WAAF to transport ground forces to incident flashpoints around the world, the Magnacopter incorporated a fully pressurised cockpit and cabin allowing it to operate in zones affected by radiation and toxic gas. Although the craft saw active service for some years it was eventually deemed too slow and impractical for combat use due to the relatively small number of troops it could carry. Unwilling to scrap an otherwise reliable and sturdy vehicle, however, the WAAF decided to repurpose it completely as a means of transport for high ranking officials, with the additional capability of functioning as a mobile command centre.

Like other WAAF and World Navy vehicles, the Magnacopter can be requisitioned for use by Spectrum at any time, and is especially useful due to its pressurised interior for flights to Cloudbase. On these occasions it is usually flown by one of the off-duty Angels, who always welcome the opportunity to pilot the seemingly cumbersome, but in reality exceptionally manoeuvrable craft.

Pioneering the design feature of variable incident tail vanes combined with rocket thrusters that was later incorporated into the Rotar helicopter, the Magnacopter can also descend by means of gliding to effect a safe landing on any terrain, or on water through the use of its high buoyancy landing floats, but as International Engineering's compressor turbine unit has never been known to fail, this capability has only been put into practice during emergency training exercises. Internally the Magnacopter is fitted out with seating for up to 20 passengers, and the cabin space includes a dining area that can be converted to a conference room. The pressurised interior also provides direct access to a small cargo hold capable of carrying an average-sized vehicle such as an MSV. In areas where the landing zone atmosphere has been compromised, this can be used to transport passengers from the Magnacopter in ultimate safety.

SPECTRUM CODE NAME :
Symphony Angel
OPERATIONAL DUTIES :
Angel Flight Pilot
REAL NAME :
Karen Wainwright
DATE OF BIRTH :
6 January 2042
PLACE OF BIRTH :
Cedar Rapids, USA

BACKGROUND : Recognised as academic high flyer while at school in Boston. Graduated to Yale University at only 16. Attained seven degrees in mathematics and technology related subjects. Immediately contacted by newly formed Universal Secret Service on graduation and enrolled on service training course. Passing in two years, entered active duty as agent specialising in industrial espionage. Brilliant handling of tricky situations led to her becoming services number one agent. Became expert pilot after training for special mission. Seeking a career in aviation, left USS to join private charter company specialising in VIP service. Talent recognised by World Security Council member travelling as passenger who recommended her to Spectrum selection committee. Immediately accepted offer to join Angel flight crew.

PERSONAL INTERESTS : Enjoys designing new hairstyles, often working alongside Destiny Angel to create new fashion looks.

MAGNACOPTER

A long-range passenger transporter originally designed for use by the World Army Air Force as a troop carrier, the Magnacopter can also transport equipment and vehicles in its cargo bay.

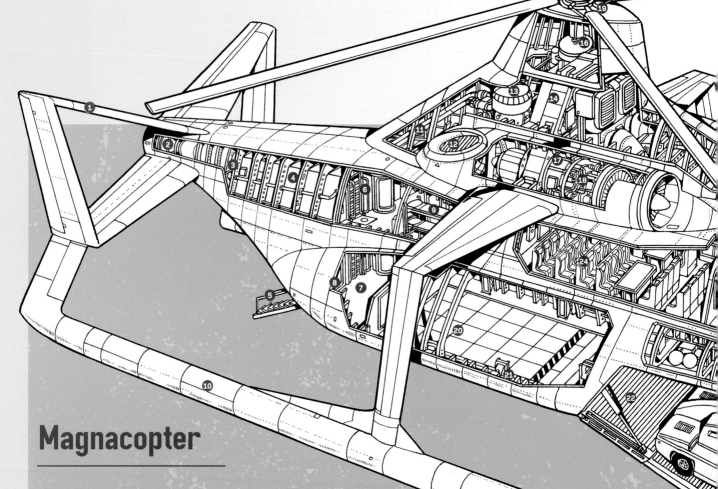

Magnacopter

1. Variable-incidence tail vanes provide maximum stability, enabling the craft to glide for some distance in the event of power failure
2. Rocket motor provides additional horizontal thrust if required
3. Fuel feed regulator
4. Fuel tanks
5. Exit hatch ladder
6. Lift and access ladder linking passenger deck to storage hold and rear exit
7. Vestibule leading to passenger deck, storage hold and exit hatch
8. Passenger exit hatch
9. Sleeping accommodation for up to four personnel making longer or overnight flights
10. High-buoyancy landing floats
11. Fuel-feed pipes
12. Turbine exhaust grille
13. Oil cooling system
14. Main rotor power-control unit
15. Rotor head
16. Gearbox
17. Starboard International Engineering WAA68 turbojet

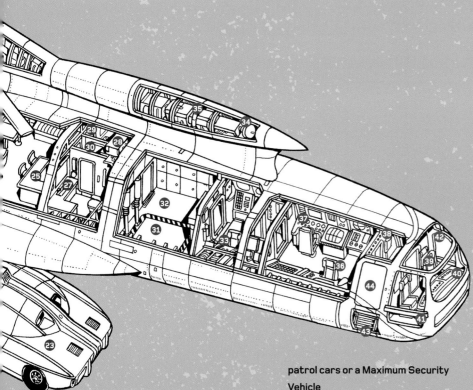

25 Food preparation area and bar

26 Eating area: can be converted to a small conference facility if required

27 Toilet and personal hygiene station

28 Shower room and additional toilet

29 Water tank

30 Central corridor

31 Cargo loading underside hydraulic lift

32 Forward cargo hold, used to transport smaller cargo items

33 Flight engineer's cabin

34 Search radar scanner

35 Avionics and flight instrument fairing

36 Communications officer's bay

37 Tactical operations instrumentation: used if the Magacopter becomes a mobile operations command centre

38 Crew entry/exit vestibule

39 Dual pilot seat

40 Instrument panel shroud

41 Jettisonable cockpit side-window panels

42 Electrically heated polarised windscreen panels

43 Exit hatch ladder in stowed position

44 Starboard crew exit hatch

18 International Engineering compressor turbine

19 Blade root attachment joint, foldable for hangar storage

20 Storage hold can be used for a variety of purposes and cargoes, including the transportation of ground vehicles, including Spectrum Pursuit Vehicles, patrol cars or a Maximum Security Vehicle

21 Variable-position electro-magnetic clamp maintains secure position of vehicle during flight. Clamps can be adjusted to fit and secure any vehicle that can fit in the stowage hold

22 Storage hold exit hatch and ramp

23 Maximum Security Vehicle

24 Passenger deck

SPACE: 2068

The conquest of space has remained one of mankind's ambitions since early successes in the late 20th century saw the establishment of satellite networks and the first lunar landings. In the aftermath of the global war of 2028, thoughts once again turned to the stars and the possibilities of space exploration and to meet this challenge the provisional World Government founded the Solar System Exploration Council. Its task – to consider the opportunities for travelling beyond the Earth and to develop new technology to aid in this quest.

The SSEC's first priority was to establish a new integrated launch facility, other rocket bases having been prime targets for destruction in the recent conflict. A site was chosen on America's west coast which offered scope for future expansion should it prove necessary. In honour of the pioneering American astronaut the new site was given the name Glenn Field and was first opened in February 2040 after construction of initial launch facilities for conventional rockets had been completed. These would primarily be intended for satellite launchings under

SPECTRUM CODE NAME :
Captain Black
OPERATIONAL DUTIES :
No longer active with
Spectrum
REAL NAME :
Conrad Turner
DATE OF BIRTH :
Information Unavailable
PLACE OF BIRTH :
Information Unavailable

BACKGROUND : Orphaned at age of seven months during atomic war of late 2020s and left in care of distant relatives. Entered Northern England's Manchester Technical Academy and gained diplomas in physics, space navigation and international law. Studied at Northern University and gained degrees in science and technology. Joined British Air Force and gained recognition for outstanding bravery during sabotage attempt at airbase. After British civil war resulted in overthrow of country's dictatorship and acceptance into membership of World Senate, joined World Army Air Force as pilot. Following formation of World Space Patrol joined service as commander of experimental XL3 spacecraft. Having recognised his progress and achievements he was the first man to be chosen by Spectrum's selection committee as a field agent. Decision ended in disaster following his selection as commander of Martian mission. Launched to investigate signals emanating from Mars, mission resulted in destruction of complex constructed by alien beings known as 'The Mysterons'. Attack on complex led to subsequent declaration of war against Earth by Mysterons.

ADDITIONAL INFORMATION : Black now believed to have been taken over by Mysterons to act as their agent on Earth.

the supervision of International Space Control, but would also enable the SSEC to launch its own exploratory probes.

Experiments were also initiated into the practical possibilities of launching a network of weather control satellites, although these ultimately ended in failure. More recently a new facility has been built at Mount Kenya by the World Weather Control Organisation to provide the launch pad for a project developed by Professor Arnold Deitz, which he claims will result in a long sought after solution to the challenge of introducing effective weather manipulation.

Following the cessation of international hostilities, and the amalgamation of the world's military forces under the auspices of the World Government, a new military body was also formed to protect Earth's interests in outer space. Named the World Solar Space Command, it would take responsibility for any military applications of space exploration and research – particularly with the development of rocket propulsion and operating systems. Currently led by Space General Peterson, the WSSC maintains a rocket research establishment at Base Concord, situated on an island off the coast of Australia, in addition to other top secret bases around the world.

Recognising the growing importance of space ventures to the world economy, a new World Government department – Space Administration – was formed specifically to deal with all aspects of space exploration and exploitation. The department would be responsible for planning, directing and funding any projects based in space in association with World Government and business interests. Manned and unmanned commercial satellite operators, including the TVR news and entertainment conglomerate, and a global network of geo-positional tracking stations became an

early source of revenue, while government-funded tele-relay networks and traffic monitoring systems also came under the responsibility of the Space Administration department.

Looking beyond the Earth's orbit, the possibilities of a return to the Moon and ultimately lunar colonisation began to be explored. The mining of mineral resources was seen as one potential reason for stepping back on to the Moon's surface, as was the consideration of its use as a dumping zone for Earth's growing deposits of toxic waste. A programme of lunar landings and the gradual establishment of habitable bases led to a full-scale programme of lunar building beginning with the construction of the first major city on the Moon, Lunarville 1, which was built to serve as a rocket launch facility in 2056. It was from here that the Neptune Probe programme was launched two years later.

This lunar development programme necessitated the construction of new facilities at Glenn Field to provide rocket transport to the satellite and led to the introduction of a series of rockets designated with the prefix 'X' (standing for exploration). The latest of these are the XK class which currently operate a regular means of transport between Glenn Field and the lunar stations for military personnel between Glenn Field under the control of pilots of the WSSC Space Patrol division, which like the XK class rockets will soon be officially superceded by the newly formed World Space Patrol. Other civilian and commercial flights to the satellite operate from a new base established in Siberia, specifically designed to cater for space freighters.

As all the elements vital to human life can be found on, or near to, the lunar surface, the development of further lunar stations was carried out, and once the great breakthrough had been made that enabled the synthesis of air and water to be achieved through the extraction of hydrogen and oxygen present on the Moon, supplies no longer needed to be transported from the Earth. This step forward also facilitated the construction of Lunarville 4, which was designed to produce almost all the

food required to feed the Moon's growing population. Further facilities constructed in Lunarville 5 and 6 finally resulted in complete self-sufficiency and an end to any reliance on Earth for survival. Since then, a further lunar station, Lunarville 7, has been built from which all lunar affairs are managed under the command of the Lunar Controller. This base now serves as administration and transport hub for Earth rockets and freighters and houses maintenance facilities for all lunar craft, which include long-range Moonmobiles and construction vehicles. Lunarville 7 is also the first of the lunar stations to be completely computer operated, its functions being controlled by a central processor known as SID (Speech Intelligence Decoder). SID answers directly to ~Lunarville personnel through the use of speech recognition discs, and although it was designed on Earth, it was built entirely on the Moon.

With a population of 4,000 now living in safety and comfort on the Moon, many of whom were initially encouraged to become settlers through the promise of self-governance and lack of interference from Earth administration, it is not surprising that

many are now calling for independence from their home planet, although no legal framework is currently in place to realise this potential eventuality. In the meantime further development of lunar habitation and mineral exploitation will continue.

Since man's return to the Moon, plans have also been put in place by the SSEC to send further manned missions into the Solar System, with the first obvious target being Mars. In conjunction with the WSSC, a Martian Exploration Centre was founded at the command's Cape Johnson base, under the authority of Space Colonel Harris. Here intensive research was carried out into the potential benefits of a Martian mission and the means by which it could be achieved. Eventually a decision was reached that the most cost effective solution would be to create a re-usable exploration vehicle that could be launched from new facilities to be built at Glenn Field. Having approved a design submitted by the New World Aircraft Corporation, construction of a new landing strip and hangars began at the spaceport in the early 2060s. With a runway 20 miles long and a computer-controlled assembly system supervised by Glenn

Field's controller Commander Casey, the new ship – named Zero X – would be ready to launch a five-man expedition to Mars in 2064, taking mankind to the red planet for the first time.

Beyond that, thoughts are turning to exploration outside the Solar System – the latest venture being Probe Omega. Due to the current lack of space at Glenn Field this will be launched from a newly constructed pad adjoining the Siberian Space Freight Base. Its destination – the Mexican Hat, or Sombrero galaxy, which will be the furthest that a vessel from Earth will have travelled beyond its home planet. Plans are also underway to construct a new space base for the recently created military organisation, the World Space Patrol, and for a space fleet to serve it, designated as 'XL' class craft. To enable these new ships to travel at three times current space velocities, they will be fitted with nose cone casings constructed from the recently discovered mineral Tritonium, deposits of which can only be found in one place on Earth – beneath the North Pole, where a sub-icepack mining base has recently started operating. With these, and other incredible new achievements, the conquest of space looks assured.

GLENN FIELD

The world's most advanced spaceport, Glenn Field operates as a base for manned and unmanned rocket launch facilities and is also now home to Zero X, the largest spaceship ever built.

Glenn Field

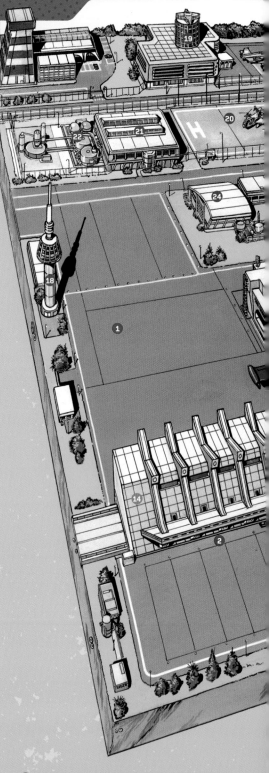

ZERO X LAUNCH ASSEMBLY

1 At the order of the Glenn Field controller, the Zero X hangar slides back to reveal the ship's main body

2 The Zero X hangar door slides downwards to allow the main body to approach the launch apron

3 Once the Zero X main body has taken up position on the launch apron, the ship is raised to enable Lifting Body 2 to clamp on to the rear of the craft

4 With the main body raised, Lifting Body 2 leaves its hangar and turns 90 degrees to clamp on to the underside of the main body

5 An overhead monorail is deployed and positioned at the front of the main body. This allows Lifting Body 1 to travel from its hangar to the launch apron, swing 90 degrees and clamp on to the topside of the main body at the front

6 With the crew already on board, the MEV detaches from the control building and is transported to the launch apron

7 The MEV swivels 90 degrees and is reversed on to the front at the main body and clamped into place

8 Finally, the nose cone is raised from its underground emplacement and transported back towards the front of Zero X, clamping into the MEV. Zero X is ready for launch

ZERO X LAUNCH ASSEMBLY ADDITIONAL DATA

9 Hydraulic lifts built into launch apron raise the main body to allow Lifting Body 2 to clamp on to the underside

10 Lifting Body 1 positioning monorail support in lowered position

11 Lifting Body 1 positioning monorail features two support stanchions that raise and briefly lower in sequence as the lifting body passes through. These support the weight of the lifting body on the rail as it travels towards the front of the main body. The stanchions are lowered again as the monorail retracts back into the Lifting Body 1 hangar once the sequence is completed

12 Lifting body positioning monorail emplacement. Each cahelium–strengthened hinged section locks into horizontal position as the monorail is deployed

13 Hydraulic lift raises nose cone on its trolley before it is transported to the front of the MEV

14 Zero X main body hangar

15 Zero X Lifting Body 2 hangar

16 Zero X Lifting Body 1 hangar

17 Glenn Field control building and main control tower

18 Interplanetary communications tower uses light refraction video correction plus Neutroni systems to provide

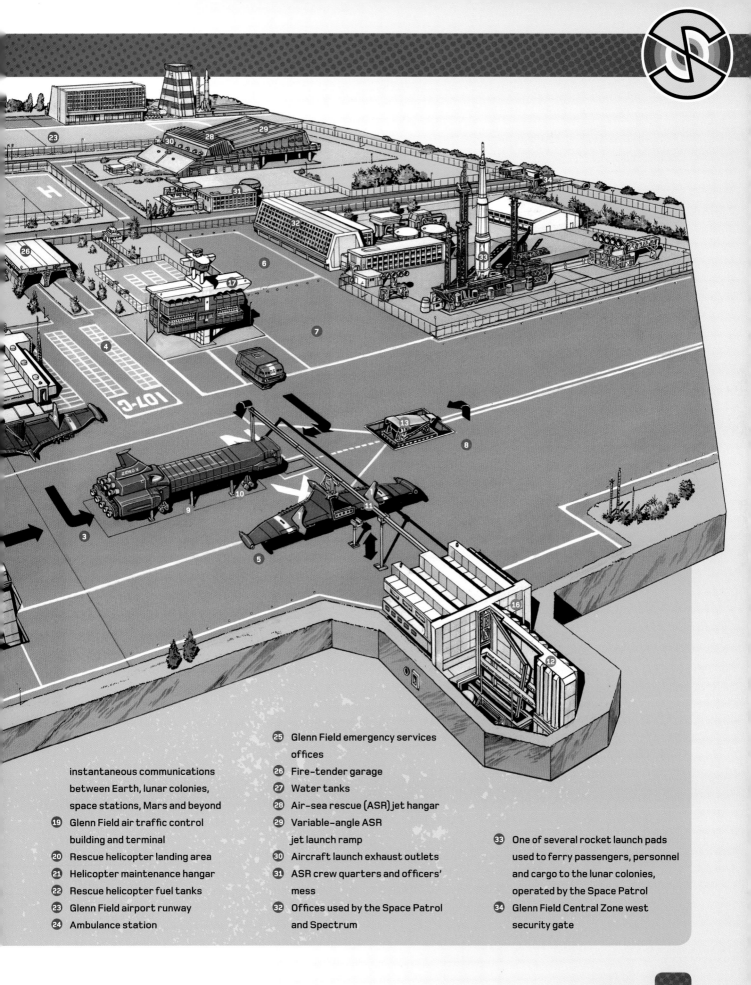

instantaneous communications
between Earth, lunar colonies,
space stations, Mars and beyond

19 Glenn Field air traffic control
building and terminal

20 Rescue helicopter landing area

21 Helicopter maintenance hangar

22 Rescue helicopter fuel tanks

23 Glenn Field airport runway

24 Ambulance station

25 Glenn Field emergency services
offices

26 Fire-tender garage

27 Water tanks

28 Air-sea rescue (ASR) jet hangar

29 Variable-angle ASR
jet launch ramp

30 Aircraft launch exhaust outlets

31 ASR crew quarters and officers'
mess

32 Offices used by the Space Patrol
and Spectrum

33 One of several rocket launch pads
used to ferry passengers, personnel
and cargo to the lunar colonies,
operated by the Space Patrol

34 Glenn Field Central Zone west
security gate

When plans to develop a sustainable interplanetary exploration programme were first announced by the Solar System Exploration Council in the early 2050s, leading aviation and engineering companies around the world were invited to submit design proposals for a reusable deep space transporter capable of providing a means of planetary landing and potentially adaptable to carry cargo. Of the designs submitted only one fully met all the criteria laid down by the SSEC.

Designated 'Zero X' (short for Zero Altitude Launch Space Exploration Craft), the revolutionary concept put forward by the New World Aircraft Corporation was to construct a craft that would take off horizontally from a conventional runway with the use of wing-shaped 'lifting bodies'. These would be detached in the upper atmosphere to allow the main body to continue into space under rocket power. Once in orbit around a selected planet an excursion vehicle forming the forward part of the main body would then separate to make a surface landing under its own power before returning to rejoin the main body. The landing craft would also be equipped with tracks to allow it to traverse the planet's surface.

Once detailed plans had been drawn up and approved in 2060, work began to build the first 'Zero X' and to construct the necessary facilities at Glenn Field spaceport for its manufacture and launch. The initial target - a manned landing on Mars in 2064. As construction continued over the following years a joint WSSC and SSEC selection committee was formed to recruit a suitably qualified crew to take up the challenge of commanding this extraordinary wonder of the 21st century.

After exhaustive tests, a senior three-man unit was chosen on the basis of their proven technical ability and psychologically compatible personal qualities. In command would be experienced space freighter pilot Paul Travers, with ex-colleague Greg Martin as co-pilot and World Air Force trained electronics expert Brad Newman as space navigator. Together the three men, in addition to a back-up crew, were put through an extensive training programme with the use of computer-controlled simulators in preparation for the scheduled first flight of Zero X in the summer of 2064.

As the world knows, since then the Zero X programme has been dogged by misfortune and disaster. Resulting from a

breach of Glenn Field's stringent security by a determined and ingenious individual, the first Martian mission ended in premature failure when the craft crash-landed in the sea shortly after take-off. Subsequent investigations concluded that this was due to the fouling of a lifting body control system during a suspected attempt by the interloper to photograph the innovative mechanisms of the lifting body control systems prior to parachuting from the lifting body while the craft was still in the Earth's lower atmosphere. Crushed footwear found lodged in a vital component by crash investigators led them to determine that this directly resulted in the crew losing control of the craft.

It is believed that the same individual was responsible for making a further attempt to gain confidential information from the Zero X project by posing as one of the scientific advisors attached to the second mission launched in 2066. Although this intrusion was detected by external security advisors assigned by the SSEC to monitor the launch, the mission itself would ultimately end in disaster as a result of damage sustained to the ship's onboard computer during a hostile encounter with fire-spitting rock snakes on the surface of Mars. This led to a malfunction in the lifting body and escape unit control systems and resulted in the ship crash-landing on the town of Craigsville on its return to Earth. Fortunately enough warning had been received to implement a total evacuation of the town, and emergency mid-air repairs to the Zero X escape capsule control unit enabled the crew and passengers to eject safely.

Now a third Zero X expedition has ended in even stranger misfortune. Launched under the command of Spectrum's Captain Black, with a three-man SSEC crew led by back-up programme pilot Lieutenant Dean, and on a mission to investigate the source of inexplicable signals emanating from Mars which were first detected during the previous planetary excursion, the Zero X Mark III returned to Earth in mysterious circumstances. In the confusion of a landing that followed a near collision with a news reporter's aircraft above Glenn Field, Captain Black inexplicably vanished from the spaceport. Of the SSEC crew that had accompanied him there was no trace, although their fate may have been connected to signs of a struggle found near one of the main body airlocks.

None of the misfortunes that have befallen the Zero X since its first launch can be attributable to the craft itself however, which has proved itself to be conceptually and technically without fault. On the strength of its proven operational track record, Captain Travers and his crew have been reassigned to the craft in the expectation that missions will continue in the future to fulfil the project's original purpose.

ZERO X DUTY CREW

COMMANDER – CAPTAIN PAUL TRAVERS
Born on America's Eastern seaboard, 36-year-old Paul Travers showed an aptitude for science at an early age and became a trainee space freighter navigator at the age of 17. Soon promoted to the position of freighter pilot, and initially employed on commercial lunar cargo services from the Siberian Space Freight Base, Travers joined the SSEC pilot training scheme as part of its first intake and due to his skill and experience was selected to be the first commander of Zero X.

CO-PILOT – CAPTAIN GREG MARTIN
A fellow employee of the Lunar Cargo Corporation, 34-year-old Hawaiian-born Greg Martin worked closely with Paul Travers for some years as a junior flight controller. Having been recommended by Travers to join the Zero X training programme, he took part in early ground tests and was unanimously selected as the senior flight crew's second in command.

SPACE NAVIGATOR – LIEUTENANT BRAD NEWMAN
At 28, Newman is the youngest member of the current Zero X crew. An electronics specialist with an in-depth knowledge of the latest space communication systems, he is also familiar with advanced navigational aids having trained as a guidance system operator in the World Air Force. As a member of the Zero X crew his secondary duty, in addition to navigation, is to man the main body of the craft to maintain it in orbit while the excursion vehicle makes planetary landfall.

ZERO X CONTROL TOWER

C ommand centre for the Zero X missions, the Zero X control tower also serves as docking port for the spaceship's manned excursion vehicle.

Control Tower

1. Control room
2. Space port controllers' Operations Command Console
3. Command Centre communications array
4. Lift shaft in which Operations Command Console is lowered to Mission Control level
5. Command Centre lift to all levels
6. Mission Control level command area and Zero X crew standby room
7. Space and Solar Exploration Committee conference room
8. Mission Control level for other services operating from Glenn Field
9. Administration offices
10. Launch control and monitoring computers and consoles
11. Mission supervisors' command booth
12. Zero X flight and life-support systems monitors: also used for other spacecraft linked to Glenn Field when Zero X is not in use
13. Spectrum liaison meeting room and offices
14. Press interview room
15. Reporters' office with videophone and electronic communication links

16. Hydraulic rams beneath the plinth on which the MEV is docked lower the craft and its carrier to ground level, beginning Stage 1 of Zero X's launch sequence
17. Martian Exploration Vehicle (MEV) in standby position prior to crew embarkation
18. Topside missile launcher
19. MEV laboratory
20. MEV control room
21. Science Officers' cockpit
22. MEV lighting and sensor array panel, below which are retro rockets and missile launcher
23. Starboard rocket thruster
24. Retracted port caterpillar track system: used for planetary surface exploration
25. Forward port landing rocket
26. MEV exit/entry airlock with integrated ladder
27. MEV life support systems
28. Escape capsule can be accessed by crew in their flight seats via the MEV's central corridor through the capsule's double doors
29. Forward capsule door
30. Rear capsule door

31. Fuel tanks
32. Rear airlock
33. MEV central access corridor: at launch, the crew are carried in their flight seats in the control tower standby room to their respective stations in the MEV, via the rear airlock and through the double-doored Emergency Escape Capsule. If required, the two-man science team follow in their seats, but turn left to the port side cockpit. Other personnel then follow to their respective stations if required

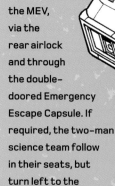

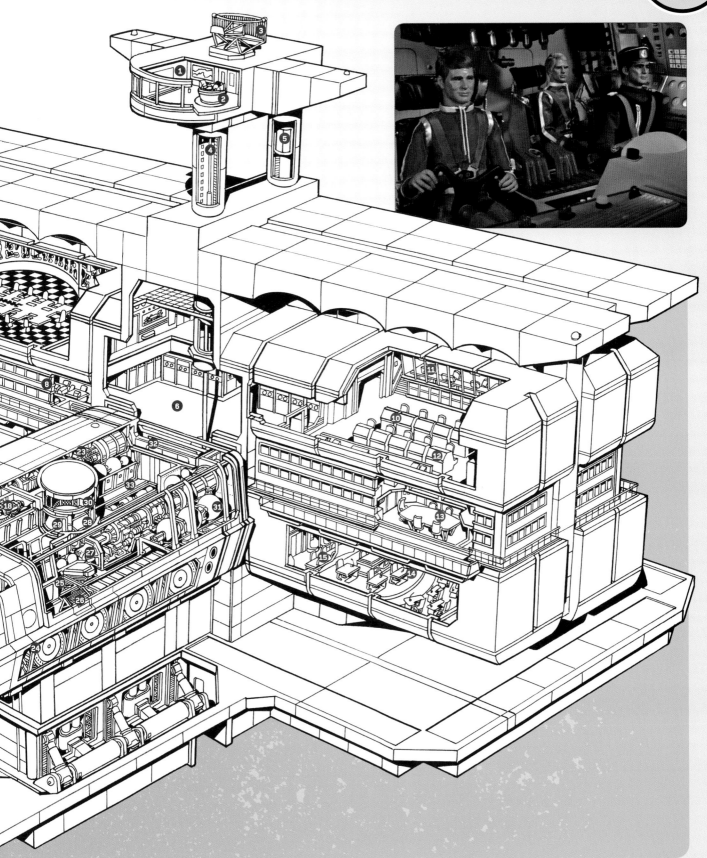

ZERO X

The dual-winged Zero X is a revolutionary concept in spaceship development, consisting of fully reusable units that enable the craft to make repeated journeys to distant planets.

Zero X
Technical data

LENGTH:	390ft
WINGSPAN:	250ft
TOTAL WEIGHT:	5,240,000lbs
TOTAL DELTA VELOCITY:	40mps

Zero X

1. Bank of five secondary variable-mode rocket engines
2. Intakes for variable-mode rocket engines. In atmospheric flight, air serves as an oxidant, leaving the Toxerlene in the fuel tanks for propulsion in space
3. Bank of three primary variable-mode chemical rocket engines operate as high-performance sustainer rockets for spaceflight and as gas-turbine jet engines in atmosphere if required
4. Air intakes serve upper bank of variable-mode engines when used as jet engines in the atmosphere
5. Electro-magnetic clamps connect Lifting Body 2 to Zero X
6. Jet engines control glide path of lifting body once detached from main body of Zero X
7. Starboard stabilising fin
8. Starboard inner aileron
9. Retracted starboard booster nacelle undercarriage
10. Ram-jet fuel tanks
11. Retracted starboard centrally mounted undercarriage
12. Ram jets propel Zero X into upper atmosphere before lifting body detaches and main chemical rockets take over
13. Lifting body jet air intakes
14. Retracted lifting body forward nose wheel
15. Lifting body avionics, auto-pilot and remote-control systems
16. Retracted aft starboard main body undercarriage
17. Toxerlene fuel tanks
18. Access and maintenance corridor
19. Fuel line distribution systems
20. Cargo hold 1 stores supplies and equipment, accessed from below
21. Cargo hold 2 stores atmospheric data probes that can be launched from the main body from planetary orbit
22. Electro-magnetic clamp connects Lifting Body 1 to Zero X
23. Recreation and conference room

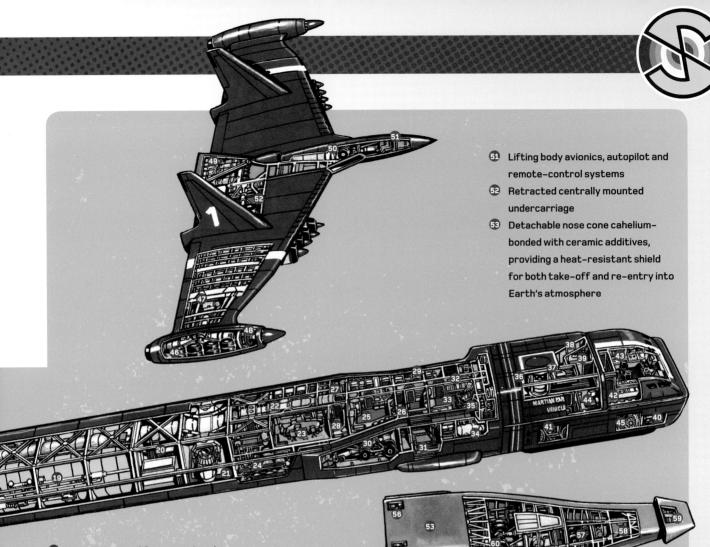

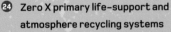

51 Lifting body avionics, autopilot and remote-control systems

52 Retracted centrally mounted undercarriage

53 Detachable nose cone cahelium-bonded with ceramic additives, providing a heat-resistant shield for both take-off and re-entry into Earth's atmosphere

24 Zero X primary life-support and atmosphere recycling systems

25 Laboratory

26 Stairwell to underside access ramp

27 Toilets, washrooms, shower cubicles

28 Galley

29 Crew quarters

30 Forward main body undercarriage

31 Access ramp to ground level

32 Main body central corridor leads to MEV via airlock

33 Main body command centre

34 Pitch and yaw rocket fuel tank

35 Main body pitch and yaw rocket booster

36 MEV emergency escape capsule

37 Topside missile launcher

38 Science team cabin access corridor

39 Medical bay

40 Forward missile launcher

41 Rear starboard landing rocket: one of four

42 Laboratory

43 MEV control room: all Zero X functions can be controlled from here, including the MEV's planetary landing operations

44 Crew quarters

45 Forward retracted caterpillar track wheel

46 Lifting Body 1 starboard booster nacelle retracted undercarriage

47 Wing-tip hinge spars: jet nacelle and wing tip folds down to ground level when Zero X lifts off

48 Wing-tip booster engine

49 Glide-path control jet engines return lifting body to the ground once detached from Zero X

50 Lifting Body 1 nosewheel

54 Starboard jet engine provides controlled thrust after detaching from Zero X in the upper atmosphere, and also for taking off to reconnect with the ship upon its return

55 Starboard electromagnetic docking clamp

56 Topside docking clamps

57 Retracted forward nosewheel

58 Computerised control systems allow nose cone to be remotely controlled from Glenn Field or Zero X

59 External environment recorders

60 Retracted main undercarriage allows nose cone to safely land after Zero X takes off and is ready for re-use when the ship returns to Earth

ZERO X FLIGHT SEQUENCE

From its hangars on Earth, to landfall on a distant planet, the Zero X spaceship passes through several phases of assembly and disassembly, enabling the craft to travel to a selected planet and return using a fixed number of components.

ZERO X FLIGHT SEQUENCE

The Zero X main body hangar door retracts and the hangar slides back ① to reveal the main body ② . This taxis forward into launch position ③ and is raised on hydraulic rams ④ . Lifting bodies 1 and 2 are attached to the main body ⑤ to complete phase one. Detaching itself from the control tower, the Excursion Vehicle is transported to a turntable in front of the main body ⑥ and reverses into position ⑦ . The streamlined nose cone is attached and all systems are go for launch ⑧ . Once in the upper atmosphere the lifting bodies are detached and return to Earth ⑨ , followed by the nose cone. On a standard mission to Mars the main body takes six weeks to reach the planet ⑩ , and take up orbit for Excursion Vehicle separation ⑪ . Using vertical thrusters the Excursion Vehicle makes planetary landing ⑫ , to carry out surface exploration.

LUNARVILLE 7

The most advanced lunar station constructed to date, Lunarville 7 is also the first to incorporate a fully functional computerised control system.

Lunarville 7

1. Living accommodation
2. Laboratories
3. Variable-gravity generator
4. Atomic fusion reactor and electricity generators
5. Life-support dome incorporates atmosphere scrubbing and recycling facilities
6. Hydroponics dome: plants expelling oxygen are used in conjunction with life-support facilities in adjacent dome
7. Water tanks
8. Waste-disposal and recycling plant
9. Solar panel
10. Access corridors incorporate services conduits between installations, walkways and a travel-car system for faster journeys between domes
11. Spaceprobe rocket launch area; little used, but still maintained
12. Main subspace/Neutroni communications antenna
13. Hospital dome
14. Emergency power plant topped by spacecraft beam guidance tower, enabling spacecraft to land at the base safely under lunar control
15. Moonmobile hangar, parts of which can be airlocked
16. Moonmobile hangar door
17. Cargo Moonmobile
18. Lunar surface vehicle garage
19. Moonmobile
20. Main landing pad
21. Airlock three
22. Earth/Moon rocket shuttle landing pad
23. Earth–Moon shuttle rocket capsule
24. Administration offices
25. Life-support services; water and air tanks, plus recycling units
26. Restaurant
27. Reception area
28. Main atrium, with shop units and leisure facilities
29. Travel car system terminus
30. Travel car
31. Entrance to underground corridor system
32. Base systems control computer interface
33. Lunar controller's office
34. Factory unit
35. Solar panel provides independent power lighting to factory
36. Factory unit leased to a number of companies manufacturing products in reduced lunar gravity environment conditions

The principal means of transport between lunar stations and for lunar excursions, Moonmobiles utilise the low gravity conditions of the Moon to make flights consisting of short, energy-saving hops.

Moonmobile Cargo Transporter

1. Rear vertical thruster; used in short bursts, the rear and forward vertical thrust rockets provide enough lift for the Moonmobile to bounce upwards and forwards from the lunar surface, in conjunction with the rear horizontal thruster (2). The Moon's reduced gravity brings the craft back down to a soft landing on the pneumatic legs ready for the next rocket burst to propel it forwards again. Later versions of the Moonmobile use short-burst thrusters only for lunar travel
2. Rear rocket provides forward thrust
3. Rear generator powers leg pneumatic systems
4. Outer rear airlock door connects to Lunarville retractable airlocks
5. Inner rear airlock door
6. Space suit air replenishment tanks
7. Spacesuit stowage
8. Door leading to the rear central corridor, with toilet/washroom and food preparation/storage area on each side, and rear airlock beyond

9. Water tank
10. Pressurised door leading to engineering deck and cargo hold below
11. Air tanks
12. Passenger cabin
13. Air recycling and scrubbing systems
14. Micro-fusion reactor provides power for life support, heat and lighting, plus leg pneumatic control systems via electricity generators
15. Forward electricity generator
16. Engineering deck
17. Cargo deck lowers to ground level to enable vehicles to be driven out or cargo unloaded
18. Access to ground level via underside exit hatch or cargo hold lowered deck and ramp
19. Extended cargo bay access ramp
20. Access to passenger cabin
21. External conditions instruments record temperature and radiation levels
22. Pilots' cabin
23. Emergency equipment stowage
24. Flight instrument console

25. Compressed-air tanks within sealed pneumatic system operate the legs' vertical motion
26. Landing leg pneumatic system provides additional lift in conjunction with vertical thruster bursts. Legs can be locked in landing position to bring craft to a halt.
27. Forward vertical thruster provides lift in timed short bursts in conjunction with rear vertical and aft-mounted forward thrusters
28. Lunar Tractor crew cabin can hold up to four personnel
29. Lunar Tractor; primarily built for demolition operations when the Lunarville bases were built

Moonmobile
Technical data

LENGTH :	74ft
WIDTH :	45ft
WEIGHT : (STANDARD VERSION) :	2.5 tons
WEIGHT (CARGO VERSION) :	4 tons
TOP SPEED :	50mph

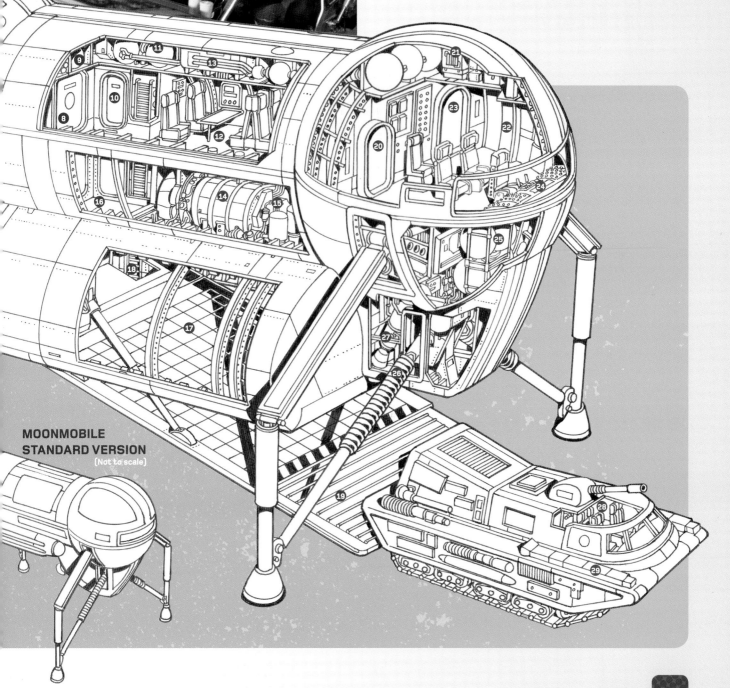

**MOONMOBILE
STANDARD VERSION**
(Not to scale)

WORLD MILITARY 2068

When the nations of the world, with a few isolated exceptions, vowed to unite following the devastating global war of 2029 and initial plans were drawn up to create a World Government with the aim of ensuring that such conflict would never again threaten the planet's inhabitants, it was deemed of primary importance to combine the military and security services of all countries into globally responsible multinational forces. During the decades that followed, and as reconstruction of damaged cities and the rebuilding of shattered communities took place, the provisional world governing council took steps to ensure this dream would become a reality. From its newly constructed Unity City base, the council would pave the way for a future World Senate, a body that would govern Earth with the over-riding aim of maintaining world peace and which, in realising this purpose, would assume ultimate control of all armed forces, although each would primarily operate under the authority of its own chief of staff and regional supreme command officers.

As this vision took shape, the gradual amalgamation of national military services began. The first armed force to be granted the official seal of a World Government charter was the World Navy. Having originally banded together to provide international famine relief in the wake of the 2029 conflict, the rag-tag remnants of once proud national fleets had soon forged themselves into an unofficial global armada which not only ensured the supply of food to starved populations, but also served as a seaborne source of medical aid. As a result, its transition into an official World Government force proved to be a relatively smooth process. Initially under the tireless command of US Navy veteran Admiral Beatty, and now led by his energetic successor Admiral Cooper Bristol, the World Navy has benefited from extensive modernisation in recent years.

Apart from the expansion of existing facilities at its Australian headquarters and its bases at Gibraltar, Hong Kong, Montevideo, New Orleans and Cape Town, an entirely new installation has been constructed in the Atlantic off the coast of Portugal. Designated Atlantica, it offers fully self-sufficient support for World Navy operations. Surrounded by a ring of defences which include banks of sea to air tracker missile launch pads and a fleet of killer submarines on constant patrol, all controlled by a fully automated master tower packed with electronics, Atlantica is designed to be completely impregnable. In addition to such extensive infrastructure renewal, the service is also introducing new vessels to its fleet to replace obsolete designs. The Clam class of submarines based on the innovative Reaper prototype, five of which have been modified and seconded to Spectrum, will soon be superseded by its recently approved successor the Barracuda. Barracuda submarines will also replace existing Clam class national submersible flagships such as the USS *Panther*. On the surface of the world's oceans further upgrades have been made to World Navy vessels which are now spearheaded by a new generation of battleships, the most advanced of which is the atomic-powered *Atlantic*.

Having taken longer to form into unified forces, the world's armies and air forces eventually began to follow their seaborne counterpart's lead, by gradually amalgamating into continental and international forces before finally evolving in the early 2050s into the World Army Air Force. Both branches of this service still maintain independent bases however to maximise operational flexibility. The World Army operates from every major country in the world, and includes atomic artillery units, hover tanks and the latest generation of Jungle Cats in its range of advanced equipment, while close co-ordination with World Air Force squadrons means that personnel and equipment can be swiftly

transported to potential combat zones at a moment's notice.

Along similar lines to the World Army's divisions, the World Air Force maintains highly efficient operational bases around the world, with its headquarters and chief testing ground located at Slaton Air Base in Canada. Here any new aircraft being considered for deployment is put through rigorous testing procedures prior to introduction into service by pilots of the World Aeronautic Society, the long-established independent advanced flying unit which also conducts training courses at the base. Among current aircraft under evaluation are the XK107 strike fighter fitted with atomic warhead equipped guided missiles, the new Skythrust airliner, which is being considered in modified form as a long-distance troop carrier, and the Goliath strategic bomber, equipped with a revolutionary prototype force field defence system. Newly approved additions to World Air Force squadrons include several squadrons of supersonic Starstriker fighters, the 'Wombat' long-range fighter carrier which allows strike aircraft to be deployed over long distances without the need for ground refueling facilities, and the B17 bomber, adapted from the versatile RTL2 rocket transporter airframe, which has already proved its versatility following its successful re-configuration for use as a civilian airliner. Like the RTL2, the B17 is based at Maxwell Airbase in Spain, adjacent to the Maxwell Field airstrip which serves the nearby Maxwell Military Rocket Development and Missile Construction Township.

Joint World Army and Air Force command is situated at Europe's largest airfield, Boscombe Down, in Southern England. WAAF Boscombe is commanded by service chief General McCormack, one of the most experienced men in the world's military. In his vast underground war room, McCormack can follow every action made by WAAF units anywhere in the world and plan strategies accordingly. Reports from reconnaissance planes on constant patrol around the globe are automatically relayed to the Boscombe War Room via their ground control monitoring stations, keeping McCormack continually informed of any likely danger hotspots and allowing him to conduct any operations necessary to eliminate potentially hazardous situations.

To add to the capabilities offered by the longer established services, specialised organisations have been established in recent years to defend mankind against new and unforeseen foes. Following the discovery of hostile sub-aquatic races dwelling beneath the oceans of the world the decision was made to form the World Aquanaut Security Patrol, a versatile force specifically charged with ensuring global security beneath the waves. Based on the west coast of the United States at its headquarters

Marineville, a fully armed self contained community that can descend into underground bunkers at the first sign of attack, the World Aquanaut Security Patrol is led by the highly decorated Commander Sam Shore, who can call on the latest submersible strike craft and jet fighter carriers, including the two-man rapid response patrol ship *Stingray* to maintain peace beneath the waves.

With the detection of signals analysed by the Nash Institute of Technology that indicate the presence of intelligent life forms in the depths of outer space, steps have also been taken to prevent possible attack from other planets and to further investigate the possible existence of other forms of life in the galaxy. Under World Army control a chain of ground to space missile bases has been installed in Canada - the Frostline Outer Space Defence System - which offers the capacity to strike against possible alien aggressors, while in the Pacific Ocean, an ultra-modern facility - Space City - has been constructed on an artificial island, not only to provide a launch pad for the newly established World Space Patrol's fleet of XL spaceships, the advanced successors of the long-serving XK rocket fleet, but also to relieve pressure on the over-stretched facilities of Glenn Field. These extra-planetary services all come under the control of Space General Peterson, senior officer of the World Solar Space Command.

Although each of these services enjoys a high degree of autonomy under the terms of their World Government charters, and act in close liaison with Spectrum whenever circumstances demand it through the offices of the world's regional defence commanders, ultimate responsibility for their day to day operational activity rests with the Supreme Commander of Earth Forces. From his command centre in New York - the Supreme Headquarters Earth Forces - and as a key member of the World Security Council, the Supreme Commander co-ordinates and directs all World Government military resources under the executive authority of the World President.

WOMBAT

Introduced into service at the 2066 British Air Show, the World Army Air Force's airborne carrier soon acquired the nickname 'Wombat'. This has now been adopted for official use.

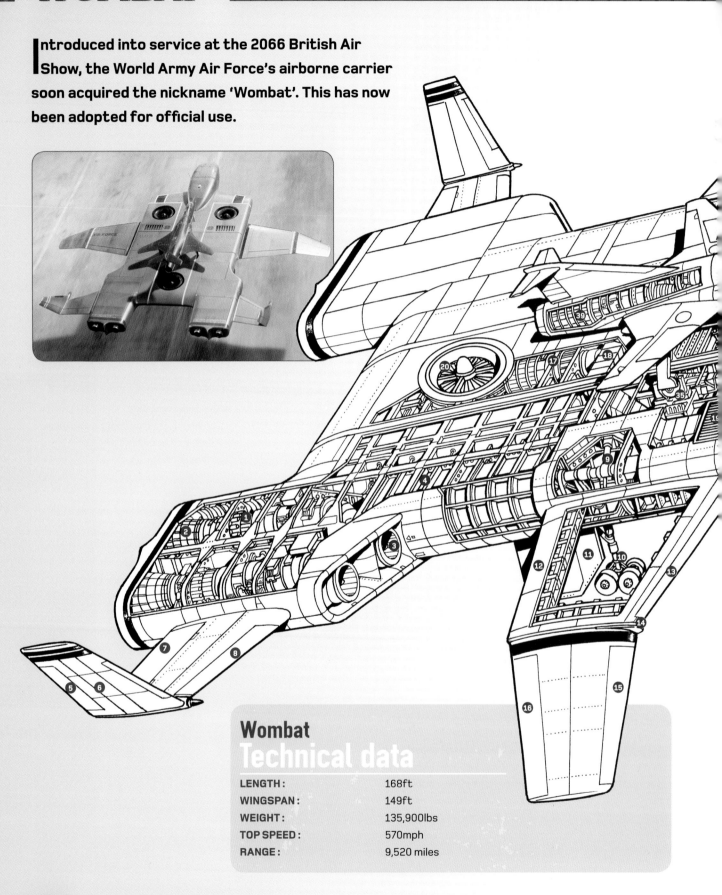

Wombat
Technical data

LENGTH :	168ft
WINGSPAN :	149ft
WEIGHT :	135,900lbs
TOP SPEED :	570mph
RANGE :	9,520 miles

Wombat overview

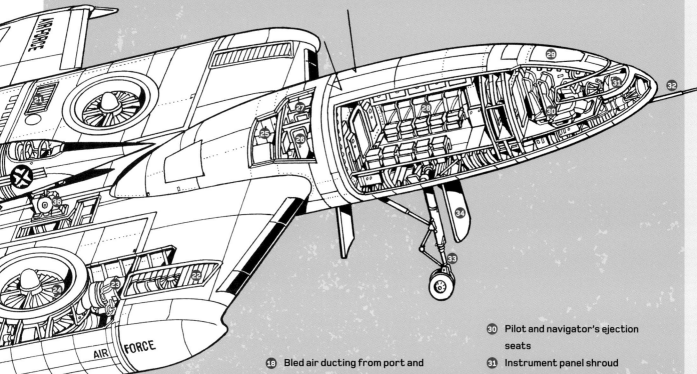

1. Starboard turbofan jet engines
2. Afterburner ducting
3. Dual air intakes serving primary turbofan jet engines
4. Fuel tanks
5. Tailfin rudder
6. Starboard tailfin
7. Tailplane aileron
8. Tailplane leading edge
9. Undercarriage hydraulics and actuators
10. Starboard undercarriage
11. Starboard undercarriage doors
12. Starboard wing aileron
13. Starboard wing leading edge
14. Starboard wing fence
15. Outer wing leading edge
16. Outer wing aileron
17. Centrally mounted rear turbine serving aft stabilising turbofan
18. Bled air ducting from port and starboard air intakes serving rear turbojet and stabilising turbofan
19. Starboard air intake serving rear turbojet and stabilising turbofan
20. Rear turbofan
21. Port air intake serving rear turbofan
22. Air intake
23. Turbine serving forward starboard stabilising turbofan
24. Port forward turbofan assists in stabilising the Wombat in air docking operations and also landing the craft on short runways
25. Supplies and equipment hold
26. Washroom and toilet
27. Supplies and equipment hold
28. Pressurised cabin used to transport up to ten personnel, or can be reconfigured for supplies and equipment storage
29. Ejection seat hatch
30. Pilot and navigator's ejection seats
31. Instrument panel shroud
32. Pitot tube
33. Nosewheel
34. Forward nosewheel door
35. Starboard docking clamp: beam guidance systems in the Dart 7 Fighter align the aircraft's undercarriage with the forward electromagnetic clamp in the raised position. Once in place, the rear clamp secures the undercarriage wheels to the Wombat's deck.
36. Forward Dart 7 undercarriage docking clamp
37. Retracted fuel feed lines linking Dart 7 to Wombat for in-flight refuelling. Power and control system conduits also connect the two aircraft so that the Wombat can be flown from the cockpit of the Dart 7 Fighter when docked
38. Dart 7 starboard engine intake
39. Dart 7 turbojet engine

RTL 2

I nitialy designed to transport military rockets constructed by the Maxwell Rocket Corporation, the RTL 2 has been modified for civilian use as a passenger airliner, and as a strategic bomber designated the B-17.

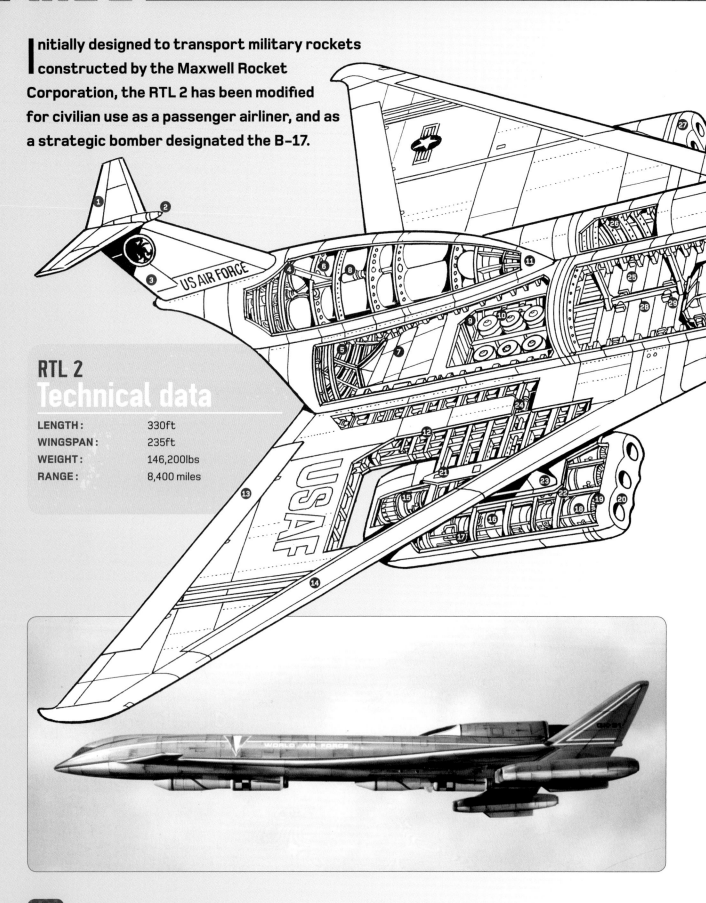

RTL 2
Technical data

LENGTH:	330ft
WINGSPAN:	235ft
WEIGHT:	146,200lbs
RANGE:	8,400 miles

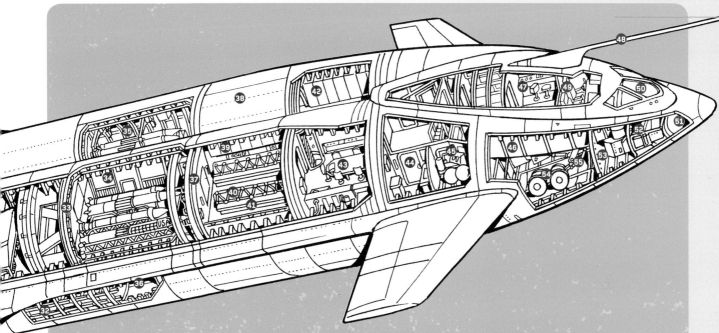

RTL 2 overview

1. Port tailplane aileron
2. Electronic countermeasures antenna
3. Tailfin rudder
4. Tailfin leading-edge rib
5. Rear cargo bay doors
6. Fuel tanks
7. Rear loading ramp
8. Fuel feed control valves and management systems
9. Mainwheel stowage well
10. Port six-wheel landing gear bogie in retracted position
11. Fuel tank containment blister
12. Integral wing fuel tanks
13. Starboard aileron
14. Starboard leading-edge wing flap
15. Centre engine exhaust duct
16. VEI turbofan jet engine
17. Oil tank
18. Engine fan blades
19. Intake centre cone

20. Starboard jet air intakes
21. Nacelle pylon attachment spars
22. Engine mounting ribs
23. Engine nacelle mounting pylon
24. Fuel feed and control management lines
25. Port aft section cargo bay provides stowage for up to six vehicles, military equipment or humanitarian supplies
26. Cargo bay light alloy construction
27. Port triple jet engine nacelle
28. Starboard aft section cargo bay
29. Cargo transit clamps
30. Vehicle/cargo in-flight transit clamps
31. World Army U87 Transporter
32. Fuselage-mounted underfloor fuel cells
33. Rear weapons by bulkhead and firewall
34. Starboard centre section weapons bay

35. Port centre section weapons bay
36. Weapons bay underside deployment/access doors
37. Forward weapons bay bulkhead and firewall
38. Port personnel/troop transportation cabin
39. Personnel equipment storage
40. Personnel seating with safety belts
41. Starboard personnel/troop transportation cabin
42. Equipment storage bay
43. Conference and strategic command area
44. Starboard personal hygiene station
45. Life-support systems bay
46. Flight deck bulkhead wall
47. Communications station
48. Pitot tube
49. Pilot and co-pilot seats
50. Instrument panel shroud
51. Radar scanner dish
52. Avionics bay
53. Avionics/electronics bay pressure bulkhead
54. Four-nosewheel landing-gear bogie: aft retracting
55. Nosewheel storage well

CLAM CLASS SUBMARINE

Clam Class Submarine
Technical data

LENGTH:	420ft
BEAM:	60ft
DISPLACEMENT:	7,000 tons
TOP SPEED:	80 knots submerged
RANGE:	Unlimited
ENDURANCE:	320 days

Spectrum operates a fleet of 6 Clam Class submarines from World Navy dockyards on global duties. The vessels are based on the original 'Reaper' prototype which first saw active service in 2066.

Clam Class Submarine

1. Sonar and aquascan systems
2. Anchor tube
3. Anchor windlass
4. Crew showers and toilets
5. Forward ballast tank inlets
6. Crew quarters
7. Forward port hydroplane
8. Forward escape hatch
9. Laundry rooms and galley
10. Airlocked missile launch bay
11. Missile storage room below airlocked launch bay
12. Sea-to-air missiles: can be fired when the submarine is either submerged or on the surface
13. Main workshop
14. Aircraft maintenance crew and pilots' offices
15. Aircraft hangar and workshop
16. Aircraft hangar hatch
17. VTOL reconnaissance aircraft
18. Aircraft lift
19. Aircraft fuel tanks
20. Torpedo launch tubes
21. Continuous delivery torpedo launch system
22. Torpedo control room
23. Junior ratings' mess
24. Ship's office
25. Lecture and tactical planning theatre
26. Topside exit hatch
27. Officer's wardroom
28. Port midships hydroplane actuators
29. Steering and control room
30. Bridge
31. Commanding officer's cabin
32. Snorkel
33. Missile control room
34. Crew quarters
35. Periscope monitor room and communications centre, relaying images and data to the bridge
36. Periscopes, radar and radio aerial retraction tubes
37. Missile launch tubes
38. Compressed-air launching cylinders
39. Missiles housed on auto-loader within armoured silo
40. High-pressure turbine
41. Low-pressure turbine
42. Engine room
43. Standby electric propulsion motor
44. Reverse gearbox
45. Port propeller shaft
46. Air recycling plant
47. Water tanks
48. Port propeller

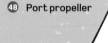

49. Fusion reactor
50. Reactor inspection hatch
51. Circulation pumps
52. Heat exchanger
53. Graphite-bonded cahelium reactor shielding
54. Aft escape hatch
55. Upper rudder segment
56. Aft hydroplane and rudder actuators

The World Navy's flagship battle cruiser, the *Atlantic* is the largest seaborne fighting vessel ever built. Powered by sea-water-cooled atomic fusion reactors, the ship can travel at a top speed of 120 knots.

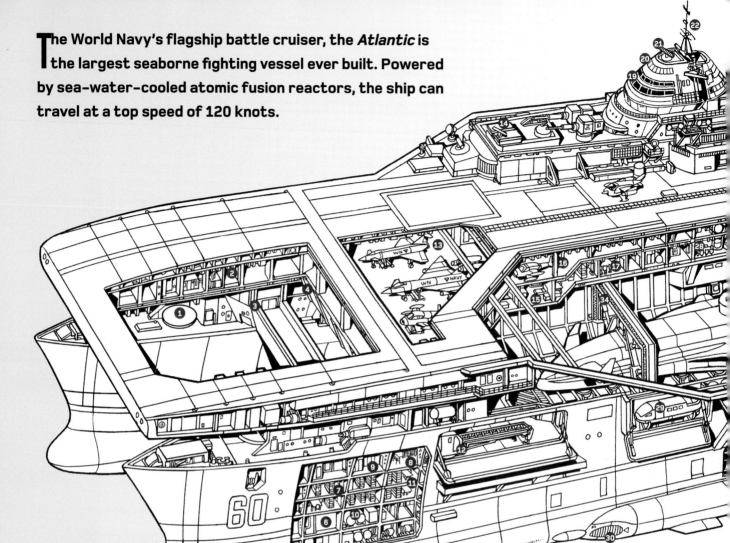

World Navy Battleship *Atlantic*
Technical data

LENGTH:	920ft
BEAM:	240ft
DISPLACEMENT:	62,000 tons
TOP SPEED:	120 knots
RANGE:	7,000 nautical miles

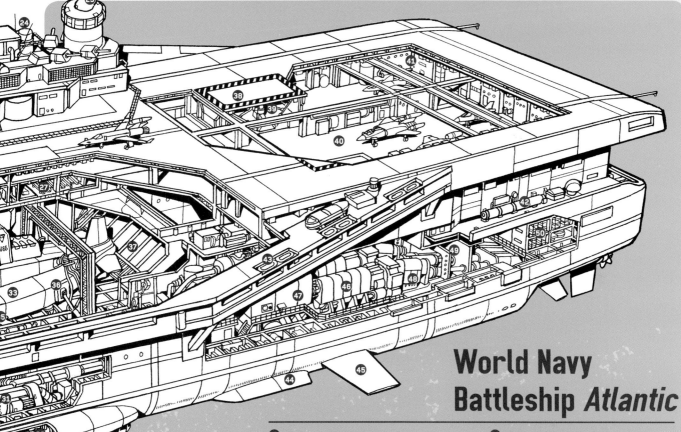

World Navy Battleship *Atlantic*

1. Starboard anchor-chain reel shroud
2. Aircraft maintenance workshops
3. Forward twin-hull support bridge, incorporating access passage to both sides of the ship
4. Flight deck underside support structure
5. Bow sonar housing
6. Stores
7. Crew quarters
8. Gymnasium
9. Changing rooms
10. Water and fuel supplies
11. Junior ratings crew mess
12. Boat davit
13. Forward hangar deck
14. Search radar
15. Senior rates quarters
16. Helijet hangar
17. Senior rates dining area
18. Forward port stabliser
19. Flying control centre
20. Bridge
21. Navigation radar
22. Wind-speed and direction anemometer
23. Main engine and gas turbine uptakes
24. VHF antennae
25. Long-range radar shroud
26. Offices
27. Lecture theatre
28. Officers' wardroom
29. Motor launch
30. Aquajet intake
31. Aquajet power unit
32. Port booster aquajet
33. World Navy/Spectrum Clam sub in Submarine Servicing Dry Dock located between the twin hulls
34. Forward docking clamp support stanchion ensures submarine is secure in rough weather
35. Submarine mid-ships docking clamp
36. Rear docking clamp
37. Dry-dock rear door
38. Aft starboard aircraft lift
39. Lift-operating hydraulic rams
40. Rear hangar deck
41. Rear deck aircraft maintenance bay and workshops
42. Inflatable life-raft storage
43. Life-raft storage
44. Bilge keel
45. Rear port stabiliser
46. Twin gas turbines
47. Atomic fusion reactors embedded within armoured graphite shielding
48. Port main gearbox
49. Gearbox output shaft to port hull propeller
50. Engineering crew quarters

ATLANTICA BASE

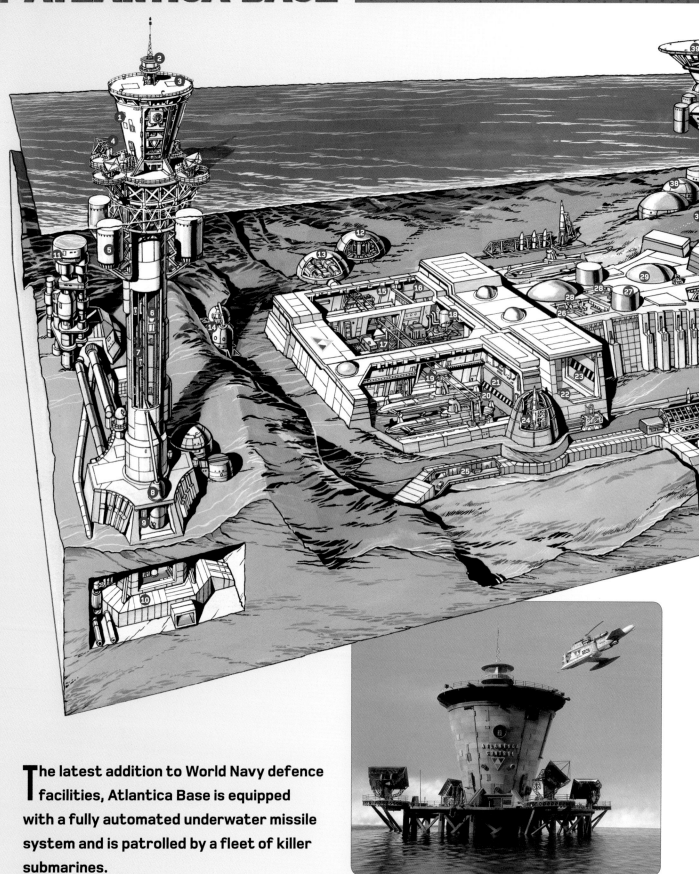

The latest addition to World Navy defence facilities, Atlantica Base is equipped with a fully automated underwater missile system and is patrolled by a fleet of killer submarines.

Atlantica Base

1. Base missile control tower: built on a ridge adjacent to the submarine servicing and missile complex, computer systems within the tower control the missile defence batteries that ring the base
2. Control observation tower
3. Access lifts to tower computer complex and the tower below
4. Radar aerial defence arrays
5. Emergency tower stabilisation turbines used in bad weather conditions
6. Service and supplies lift
7. Personnel lifts
8. Tower air supply tank
9. Laboratories and workshops
10. Tower access tunnels leading to defence ring installations and submarine servicing complex
11. Water desalination and purification plant
12. Armoured fusion reactor dome provides the primary power source for the base
13. Power turbines linked to adjacent reactor
14. Air-from-water life-support back-up systems unit
15. Submarine dry dock
16. Dry Dock 1 airlock
17. Maintenance workshops and component manufacturing plant
18. Airlock water pumping system
19. Maintenance crane
20. Submarine Dry Dock 2: two Clam class submarines can be maintained at once, either raised on hydraulic clamps or floating if the dock is partially filled
21. Inner dry dock airlock door

22. Adjustable maintenance clamp rails: submarines are electronically guided on to docking clamps within the airlock prior to water being pumped out. Once empty, the craft are carried through the dry dock for maintenance
23. Outer airlock door
24. Armoured missile engine testing silo
25. Underground installation access tunnels
26. Escape pods
27. Air purification units
28. Personnel accommodation and administration offices
29. Air storage tanks
30. Observation tower
31. Submarine crew accommodation, officers' mess, dining and recreation facilities
32. Sea-water-powered turbine
33. Defence battery missile silo
34. Atlantica missile defence battery
35. Long-range rocket in launch position
36. Airlocked launch silo
37. Rocket storage silo
38. Base supplies storage doors
39. Atlantica base primary helijet landing pad; provides access to base via lifts for personnel and supplies in addition to using submarines
40. Command centre
41. Submarine control tower
42. Submarine crew accommodation, officers' mess, dining and recreation facilities
43. Base defence sonar arrays

UNITRON TANK

A remote-controlled, fully automated, high-speed armoured fighting vehicle, the Unitron has been developed to operate in potential conflict zones around the world.

Unitron Tank
Technical data

LENGTH (GUN FORWARD):	30ft
WIDTH:	12ft
WEIGHT:	48 tons
SPEED:	60mph
ARMOUR:	Ceramic-Cahelium composite

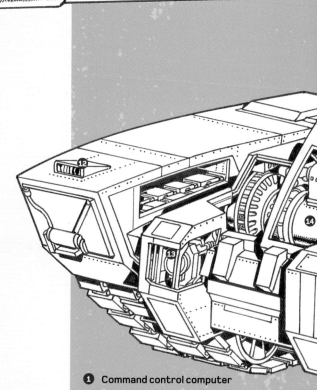

1 Command control computer system maintenance access panels. Technicians can access the computer systems via a hatch forward of the turret

2 Gyroscopically stabilised fire-control system enables the gun barrel to rotate 180 degrees vertically, and 360 degrees horizontally, allowing accurate aiming at any ground or airborne target no matter how violently the tank moves

3 Variable-mode automatic ammunition loader can operate whilst gun-barrel angle vertically rotates up to 180 degrees and in any direction

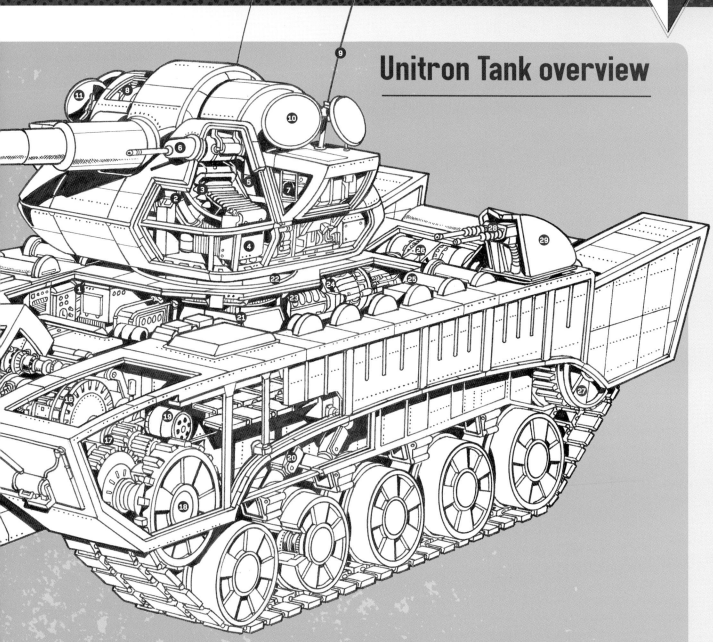

Unitron Tank overview

4 Ammunition magazine

5 Flame-thrower chemical tank

6 Flame thrower

7 Turret camera

8 Rotation-control gyroscope

9 Short-range command control antenna

10 Long-range armoured remote-control antennae receive command signals from ground-control installations via military satellite links

11 Standby long-range control antennae

12 Headlight and starboard forward camera

13 Forward sensor array

14 Gearbox

15 Brake control systems

16 Brake

17 Transmission final gear

18 Drive sprocket

19 Return roller

20 Suspension crank

21 Turret turntable control power unit

22 Turret turntable

23 Fuel cells

24 Gas-turbine servicing rear and front drives

25 Engine air filters

26 Rear drive gearbox

27 Secondary geared drive sprocket, controlled from rear drive

28 Port twin machine guns

29 Revolving gun turret

Following the fateful first mission of the Zero X Mark II to Mars, scientists were quick to examine the onboard flight recorder jettisoned with the crew aboard the ship's escape capsule as it was ejected from the crash-landing vehicle. The reported evidence of primitive life forms on the Martian surface attracted their immediate attention, but on closer analysis, previously unnoticed signals were also found to have registered on the ship's environmental sensors. Using revolutionary new interstellar monitoring equipment developed by Lieutenant Green of Spectrum in association with the world renowned Nash Institute of Technology, which had been installed aboard Spectrum's network of communication satellites, the presence of the signals was confirmed and the location of their

transmission pinpointed to a certain area of Mars. Under the command of senior Spectrum officer Captain Black, a third Zero X mission was launched to investigate the source of the signals.

Exactly what happened on Mars during the course of Black's mission, or during its return journey to Earth will probably never be known, as evidence from the flight recorders presents only an incomplete account of events. Recordings do show that following a successful planetary landing the Martian Excursion Vehicle proceeded to survey the area where the source of the signals had been detected. As these survey patrols continued senior SSEC crew member Lieutenant Dean recorded a growing sense of unease and nervousness among the crew. Theories have been proposed that these sensations and resultant behaviour may have been caused by psychic vibrations emanating from the signal's source, affecting the men's psychic well-being and affecting their ability to make rational decisions. Whatever the cause, the crew's judgement was certainly clouded when they reached their final destination. Pictures from the Zero X onboard cameras record what happened next.

Having discovered an astonishing alien complex in a valley beneath them, Captain Black and his crew lost their nerve and made an ill-judged pre-emptive attack on the installation when they saw apparently suspicious-looking devices turning towards them. Subsequent events were even more incredible. Having to the best of their knowledge destroyed the complex, they were amazed to see a ray of strange light play over the ruins while

an eerie message came through the excursion vehicle's radio receivers identifying its sender as 'The Voice of the Mysterons'. Demonstrating the claim that its source possessed the power of 'retro-metabolism' through the incredible reconstruction of its ruined complex, the alien intelligence then went on to state that retaliation for the attack would be taken against the Earth, that one of the Zero X crew would be brought under Mysteron control, and that the first act of Mysteron retaliation would be to assassinate the World President. This was man's first encounter with the strange alien power that can be heard but not seen, and which since then has made repeated attempts to carry out its threat.

From the day that this threat to Earth and its inhabitants was first realised, continued efforts have been made to discover the secrets of this mysterious force and find means to counter its attacks against our planet. Following the decision by the World Government to assign Spectrum to deal exclusively with the Mysterons' activities, detailed records have been kept of each incident involving their influence and the nature of the powers they have displayed. In the course of these incidents various innocent people have been killed and reconstructed to become Mysteron agents in order to carry out their threats. Some of these reconstructed men and women appear to have been the victims of accidents - or apparent accidents, as it is unclear whether Mysteron influence might extend to engineering a burst tyre that might cause a car to crash, or a loose chain on a diving submarine that might snare a man's foot. Some of the victims have themselves clearly been the victim of deliberate assassination, their subsequently discovered bodies, or the vehicles they were travelling in, having clearly been subjected to gunfire. On many occasions the man who the Mysterons designated as their agent on Earth - Captain Black - was witnessed in the vicinity of a victim's death, and his role as an instrument - or conductor - of his masters' powers is clearly apparent in many cases. Reports suggest that in some cases the Mysterons may also be able to transmit their powers directly to take over a potential victim without first having to kill them, and that other powers enable them to dematerialise their agents when they are trapped.

The exact rationale behind the Mysterons' at times illogical behaviour has also been questioned. On occasion assassination attempts have been abandoned for unknown reasons in favour of a victim's abduction, while the nature of the 'war of nerves' they have declared appears to be irrational and unfocused, and the use to which they put their powers poses a question mark over the serious nature of their intent. This has led many scientists on Earth to suggest that the Mysterons may not actually be sentient beings, but some form of computer-controlled entity, programmed to carry out certain actions, but unable to respond to rational argument.

Since their presence was first made known progress has been made towards answering some of these questions, and finding potential means of defence against their threats. The accidental discovery that a Mysteron agent is impervious to X-rays has led to the development of an X-ray-based Mysteron detector, and the same agent's destruction by electrocution has resulted in the creation of short- and long- range electrode ray weapons effective against a Mysteron-controlled person. Further discoveries were made after it was found that the Mysterons had established a base on the Moon, a development possibly connected to their having taken over the Lunar Controller and his assistant, whose bodies were subsequently discovered in an apparently genuinely wrecked Moonmobile piloted by a technician from Lunarville 6. Investigations of the city carried out by Spectrum revealed that it was powered by a crystal pulsator, believed to have been left embedded in a reception chamber beneath the lunar surface, and that after activation by one of the Mysterons' newly reconstructed lunar agents proceeded to initiate construction of a complex on the Moon through the three-dimensional transmission of components and materials from the Mysterons' Martian complex.

Whatever the nature and ultimate purpose of the Mysterons might be, it has been agreed that the only answers will be found on Mars, and to this end, and despite recent setbacks with attempts to launch a monitor probe a new mission - Project Sword - has been instigated. This project is to be discussed in detail at the forthcoming conference at Lake Toma in Italy, to be attended by the World President, and at which his leading scientific advisor Dr Ernst Conrad will put forward proposals that will determine Earth's return to the red planet. Until then, the people of the world can only wonder what the Mysterons actually are, whether they do in fact exist, or if there is any chance that we will ever discover their secrets.

MYSTERON LUNAR COMPLEX

Discovered by Spectrum agents during a mission to investigate reports of Mysteron communication with Lunarville 7, this complex was found to be under construction in lunar crater 101. Further investigations revealed that at its centre was a pulsator of unknown composition. Could such pulsators be the source of the Mysterons' power?

Mysteron Lunar Complex

1. Pulsator crystal: the heart of the complex and the key/beacon left behind on the Moon from an earlier Mysteron expedition. Remotely activated from Mars, construction began on power and manufacturing plants, plus other installations in readiness for the Mysterons to return and physically occupy the complex

2. Pulsator crystal containment enclosure

3. Power plant, activated by pulsator crystal to enable complex to be created

4. Zero-gravity well

5. Artificial/variable gravity generator provides gravity-free access to pulsator crystal

6. Defence drone enclosure

7. Base construction vehicles

8. Atmosphere containment and preparation tank: life-support systems held in readiness for the Mysterons' return

9. One of several structures created to provide accommodation for the returning Mysterons

10. Sub-space communications and data retrieval array linking the lunar complex with Mars

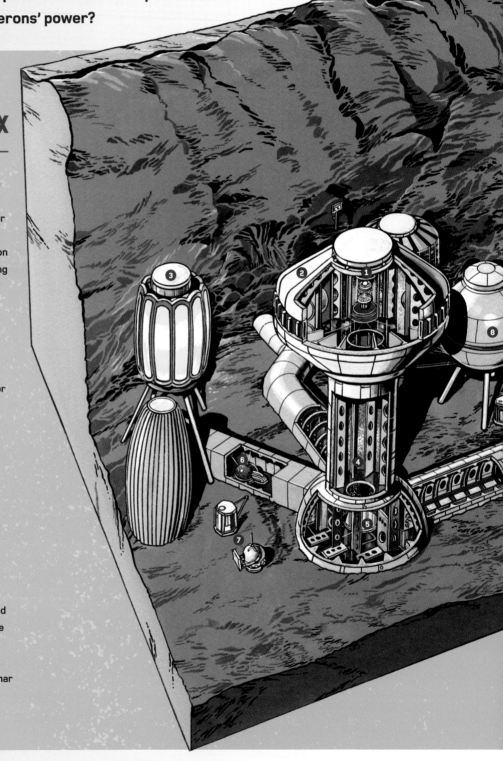

11 Manufacturing complex creates machinery, vehicles and building construction services, raw materials and technology

12 Base construction lighting

13 Secondary power plant

14 Base defence command drone

15 Base defence drone

16 Base construction vehicle

17 Servicing and construction monorail system

18 Construction raw materials carrier

19 Tunnel and track carved into crater wall by construction machines, later used by Spectrum investigation team

SPECTRAFILES

SPECTRAFILE DATABASE

Following the catastrophic events that took place on Mars earlier this year, Spectrum has been tasked with countering a significant number of threats initiated by the alien beings known as the Mysterons. In these files are details of incidents arising from a selection of these threats and the action taken. In all but the minority of cases these actions have proven Spectrum's ability to meet with exceptional efficiency the challenges our organisation has faced. I commend all our agents and operatives for their part in the execution of their duties during the course of these incidents.

Colonel White, Cloudbase, 2068

SPECTRAFILE CODE
The Mysterons Incident 1

MYSTERON ACTIVITY

MYSTERON THREAT: 'Our first act of retaliation will be to assassinate your World President'

MYSTERON FORCES: Captain Brown

SPECTRUM RESPONSE

PERSONNEL MOBILISED: Angel Crew (Destiny, Harmony, Rhapsody), Captain Brown, Captain Scarlet, Spectrum New York Security Unit

EQUIPMENT DEPLOYED: Angel Flight, Spectrum Helicopter, Security Convoy consisting of two Spectrum Saloon Cars and Maximum Security Vehicle

INCIDENT FILE

INCIDENT ZONE: New York City

INCIDENT REPORT: Following Mysteron assassination threat, Captain Brown assigned to escort World President to Spectrum Maximum Security Building New York. When Captain Brown revealed to be explosive self-detonating Mysteron-controlled replica, President deploys rapid emergency ejection system in underground office to escape subsequent destruction of security building.

SPECTRAFILE CODE
The Mysterons Incident 2

MYSTERON ACTIVITY

MYSTERON THREAT: See Incident One

MYSTERON FORCES: Captain Black, Captain Scarlet, Spectrum Helicopter A42

SPECTRUM RESPONSE

PERSONNEL MOBILISED: Angel Crew (Destiny, Rhapsody, Duty Angel), Captain Blue, Captain Scarlet

EQUIPMENT DEPLOYED: Angel Flight, Spectrum Passenger Jet, Spectrum Helicopter A42, Spectrum Pursuit Vehicle A69

INCIDENT FILE

INCIDENT ZONE: Southern England

INCIDENT REPORT: Assigned to escort World President to London in SPJ, Captain Scarlet discovered to be Mysteron replica. Pursued by Captain Blue in SPV, Scarlet proceeds to rendezvous with Mysteron-controlled Spectrum Helicopter A42 at top of London Car-vue sky-park. Angel Flight air strike against helicopter causes it to collide with structure, resulting in its destruction. President rescued by Blue with aid of thruster pack while replica Scarlet falls to ground.

INCIDENT NOTE: Following fall, Mysteron influence over Scarlet replicant lost while duplicated human characteristics and Mysteron qualities of virtual indestructibility retained. After full security clearance checks, Scarlet passed to resume duties as Spectrum agent.

SPECTRAFILE CODE
WINGED ASSASSIN

MYSTERON ACTIVITY

MYSTERON THREAT: 'We will assassinate the Director General of the United Asian Republic'

MYSTERON FORCES: Captain Black, Stratojet DT19

SPECTRUM RESPONSE

PERSONNEL MOBILISED: Angel Crew (Destiny, Harmony, Rhapsody), Captain Blue (Plan B Field Commander), Captain Grey (Plan A Field Commander), Captain Scarlet, Double for Director General, Spectrum Agents Airport Security Detail

EQUIPMENT DEPLOYED: Angel Flight, Spectrum Passenger Jet, Spectrum Pursuit Vehicle 105, Decoy Motorcade consisting of two Spectrum Saloon Cars and Maximum Security Vehicle, Yellow Fox Covert Security Transporter

INCIDENT FILE

INCIDENT ZONE: London, England

INCIDENT REPORT: Spectrum assigned to provide security while Director General of United Asian Republic on state visit to London. Security Plan A Agents successfully prevent assassination attempt at Nelson Hotel. Security Plan B provides effective protection for journey to London International Airport but despite efforts by Captain Scarlet to disable undercarriage, collision with Mysteron-controlled passenger jet during take-off results in destruction of Director General's jet and death of all on board.

SPECIAL NOTE: Captain Scarlet reports sense of unease triggered by presence of Mysteron forces. Doctor Fawn suggests this could be side effect of recent Mysteronisation. Unable to assess whether this might be permanent condition.

SPECTRAFILE CODE
BIG BEN STRIKES AGAIN

MYSTERON ACTIVITY

MYSTERON THREAT: 'Our next act of retaliation will be to destroy the city of London'

MYSTERON FORCES: Captain Black, Atomic Device Transporter

SPECTRUM RESPONSE

PERSONNEL MOBILISED: Angel Crew (Harmony, Symphony and one other), Captain Blue, Captain Grey, Captain Ochre, Captain Scarlet

EQUIPMENT DEPLOYED: Angel Flight, Spectrum Saloon Cars, Spectrum Pursuit Vehicle (unclassified)

INCIDENT FILE

INCIDENT ZONE: London, England

INCIDENT REPORT: High destruction ratio nuclear device transporter hi-jacked by Mysteron powers and driven by remote control to underground car park. Driver Macy discovered during search of city and reports having seen device activated to explode in 12 hours after believing Big Ben clock to have struck 13. Potential locations of car park identified after analysis of driver's report by Captain Blue. Transporter located and driven by Captain Scarlet to subterranean construction site for safe detonation. Scarlet sustains potentially fatal injuries while returning to ground level, but later makes full recovery.

SPECTRAFILE CODE
MANHUNT

MYSTERON ACTIVITY

MYSTERON THREAT: No threat issued

MYSTERON FORCES: Captain Black, Stone Point Village Spectrum Agent

SPECTRUM RESPONSE

PERSONNEL MOBILISED: Angel Crew (Symphony and two others), Captain Blue, Captain Grey, Captain Ochre, Captain Scarlet, Detector Truck Operators, Spectrum Ground Forces

EQUIPMENT DEPLOYED: Angel Flight, Spectrum Saloon Cars, Maximum Security Vehicle, eight Detector Trucks

INCIDENT FILE

INCIDENT ZONE: Culver Atomic Centre and surrounding area, England

INCIDENT REPORT: Following a break-in at Culver Atomic Centre, Captain Black is positively identified after being recorded by security cameras. Due to his exposure to low yield radiation during the course of the break-in, operation mounted to locate and apprehend him with the aid of directional Geiger counters. After killing local Spectrum agent who then attempts to shoot Captains Blue and Scarlet during course of search operation, Black is forced to abandon his plan to escape in SPV 0782 due to Spectrum roadblocks. Misguided initiative on the part of Symphony Angel to personally capture Black results in her being used as decoy to allow him to elude capture.

SPECTRAFILES

SPECTRAFILE CODE
POINT 783 Incident 1

MYSTERON ACTIVITY

MYSTERON THREAT: 'We will destroy the Supreme Commander of Earth Forces'

MYSTERON FORCES: Major Brooks, MCA Lorry Driver

SPECTRUM RESPONSE

PERSONNEL MOBILISED: Angel Crew (Destiny, Harmony, Melody), Captain Blue, Captain Scarlet

EQUIPMENT DEPLOYED: Angel Flight, Spectrum Passenger Jet

INCIDENT FILE

INCIDENT ZONE: Supreme Headquarters Earth Forces

INCIDENT REPORT: After escorting Supreme Commander Earth Forces to Supreme Headquarters New York for conference, Captain Scarlet prevents assassination by self-combusting Mysteron replica of Major Brooks after sensing possible Mysteron presence. Investigations subsequently reveal Brooks to be victim of accident caused by Mysteron agent in Grand Catskill Tunnel while travelling to New York with Colonel Storm (See Spectrafile Point 783 Incident Two).

SPECTRAFILE CODE
POINT 783 Incident 2

MYSTERON ACTIVITY

MYSTERON THREAT: See Incident One

MYSTERON FORCES: Captain Black, Colonel Storm

SPECTRUM RESPONSE

PERSONNEL MOBILISED: Angel Crew (Destiny, Harmony, Melody), Captain Blue, Captain Scarlet

EQUIPMENT DEPLOYED: Angel Flight, Spectrum Pursuit Vehicle 428

INCIDENT FILE

INCIDENT ZONE: Sahara Desert

INCIDENT REPORT: Captain Blue escorts Supreme Commander Earth Forces to Point 783 security blockhouse to view demonstration of Unitron tank. Tank found to have been reprogrammed after targeting blockhouse. Captain Scarlet assigned to transport Supreme Commander to safety by SPV in company of Colonel Storm while Angel flight mounts diversionary attack on Unitron. Colonel Storm proves to be Mysteron and attempts to prevent escape attempt by shooting Scarlet. Scarlet ejects himself and Supreme Commander from SPV, leaving vehicle to be destroyed by Unitron. Suffering potentially fatal injuries, Scarlet is airlifted to Cloudbase by helicopter, where he makes full recovery.

SPECTRAFILE CODE
OPERATION TIME

MYSTERON ACTIVITY

MYSTERON THREAT: 'Our next act of retaliation will be to kill time. We will kill time'

MYSTERON FORCES: Captain Black, Doctor Theodore Magnus

SPECTRUM RESPONSE

PERSONNEL MOBILISED: Destiny Angel, Captain Blue, Captain Grey, Captain Ochre, Captain Scarlet

EQUIPMENT DEPLOYED: Angel Two, Spectrum Passenger Jets

INCIDENT FILE

INCIDENT ZONE: London England, Cloudbase

INCIDENT REPORT: Worldwide alert sent out to all Spectrum agents following Mysteron transmission to ascertain exact nature of latest threat. News monitored by Captain Magenta identifies likely target as General Tiempo of Western Region World Defence due to undergo brain surgery by Doctor Theodore Magnus at Westbourne Clinic, London. Captain Scarlet assigned to escort Tiempo and Magnus to Cloudbase to ensure operation will be carried out under maximum security conditions. When radiographer discovers that Magnus is impervious to X-rays he is revealed to be Mysteron agent and attempts to escape. Cornered in Cloudbase power plant he is killed by electrocution. As a result of these developments Spectrum instigates research into feasibility of producing Mysteron detector and Anti-Mysteron weapon.

SPECTRAFILE CODE
RENEGADE ROCKET

MYSTERON ACTIVITY

MYSTERON THREAT: 'We are going to launch one of your own incendiary rockets and you will have no way of knowing its target'

MYSTERON FORCES: Captain Black, Space Major Reeves

SPECTRUM RESPONSE

PERSONNEL MOBILISED: Angel Crew (Harmony, Melody, Rhapsody), Captain Blue, Captain Scarlet

EQUIPMENT DEPLOYED: Angel Flight

INCIDENT FILE

INCIDENT ZONE: Base Concord Rocket Installation

INCIDENT REPORT: After killing rocket controller at Base Concord, Mysteron replica of Space Major Reeves programs launch of Variable Geometry Rocket with an incendiary warhead before escaping with VGR Flight Programme Unit aboard J17 fighter aircraft. Angel flight launched to intercept Reeves and retrieve VGR FPU. During air battle Reeves' aircraft destroyed as a result of deliberate crash dive. One Angel aircraft also lost in action, pilot ejected safely. Captains Blue and Scarlet assigned to effect auto-destruct of VGR with replacement FPU. Captains threatened with court martial after refusing to abandon mission when target revealed to be Base Concord. Last-minute destruction of VGR later found to be caused by activation of original FPU located in wreckage of J17.

SPECTRAFILE CODE
WHITE AS SNOW Incident 1

MYSTERON ACTIVITY

MYSTERON THREAT: 'Our next act of retaliation will be to kill the Commander-in-Chief of Spectrum, Colonel White. Do you hear, Earthmen? We will kill Colonel White'

MYSTERON FORCES: Captain Black, TVR-17 Communications Satellite

SPECTRUM RESPONSE

PERSONNEL MOBILISED: Angel Crew (Symphony)

EQUIPMENT DEPLOYED: Angel One

INCIDENT FILE

INCIDENT ZONE: Orbital Control 3, Airspace Above Cloudbase

INCIDENT REPORT: After overpowering director of Orbital Control 3 satellite operations room, Captain Black engineers destruction and subsequent Mysteronisation of TVR -17 communications satellite by programming it into catastrophic atmospheric re-entry. Reconstruction of satellite detected on crash course with Cloudbase three hours later. Reconstruction successfully destroyed by Symphony Angel under orders from Colonel White, despite objections from Captain Scarlet due to lack of Mysteron control confirmation.

SPECTRAFILE CODE
WHITE AS SNOW Incident 2

MYSTERON ACTIVITY

MYSTERON THREAT: See Incident One

MYSTERON FORCES: Soames

SPECTRUM RESPONSE

PERSONNEL MOBILISED: Captain Scarlet

EQUIPMENT DEPLOYED: No Major Equipment Deployed

INCIDENT FILE

INCIDENT ZONE: Western Atlantic

INCIDENT REPORT: After failure of Mysteron attempt to destroy Cloudbase through use of TVR-17 satellite Colonel White leaves for undisclosed destination to prevent further attacks on HQ. Acting under own initiative Captain Scarlet conceals himself aboard USS submarine *Panther II* after ordering Lieutenant Green to reveal details of White's plan to take refuge aboard vessel. Scarlet prevents further Mysteron attempt to carry out threat by securing superior in cabin locker and presenting himself as target. Court martial against Scarlet on charges punishable by death of gross insubordination dropped due to anticipated ineffectiveness of firing squad.

SPECTRAFILES

SPECTRAFILE CODE
SEEK AND DESTROY

MYSTERON ACTIVITY

MYSTERON THREAT: 'We intend to kill one of the Spectrum Angels'

MYSTERON FORCES: Captain Black, Fleet of Unmodified Viper Fighters

SPECTRUM RESPONSE

PERSONNEL MOBILISED: Angel Crew (Harmony, Melody, Rhapsody), Captain Blue, Captain Scarlet

EQUIPMENT DEPLOYED: Angel Flight, Spectrum Passenger Jet, Spectrum Saloon Car

INCIDENT FILE

INCIDENT ZONE: Northern France

INCIDENT REPORT: Captains Blue and Scarlet assigned to escort Destiny Angel to safety of Cloudbase following reception of Mysteron threat. While travelling to airport, party attacked en route by fleet of Mmysteronised Viper aircraft. Following aerial battle all Mysteronised aircraft destroyed. One Angel aircraft lost in action, pilot ejected safely.

SPECTRAFILE CODE
SPECTRUM STRIKES BACK

MYSTERON ACTIVITY

MYSTERON THREAT: 'We know of your pathetic attempts to discover our secrets, but you will never succeed. You will never solve the mystery of the Mysterons'

MYSTERON FORCES: Captain Black, Captain Indigo

SPECTRUM RESPONSE

PERSONNEL MOBILISED: Colonel White, Captain Blue, Captain Scarlet

EQUIPMENT DEPLOYED: No Major Equipment Deployed

INCIDENT FILE

INCIDENT ZONE: Base Zebra, Central Africa

INCIDENT REPORT: Colonel White, Captain Blue and Captain Scarlet attend demonstration of new Anti-Mysteron devices at Spectrum Intelligence Agency maximum security conference centre with World President, Doctor Giardello and Space General Peterson. Following demonstration in sub-surface conference room of new Mysteron detector, Captain Indigo discovered to be Mysteron agent. Trapping party with exception of Scarlet in conference room by locking it in descent mode, Indigo escapes with control unit electronic key. Scarlet pursues Indigo armed with new Anti-Mysteron gun to retrieve key. After effective test of new weapon, Scarlet retrieves key and effects release of trapped conference attendees.

SPECTRAFILE CODE
AVALANCHE

MYSTERON ACTIVITY

MYSTERON THREAT: 'Within the next four hours we will destroy key links in your Frost Line outer space defence system'

MYSTERON FORCES: Frost Line Maintenance Engineer

SPECTRUM RESPONSE

PERSONNEL MOBILISED: Angel Crew (Destiny, Harmony, Rhapsody), Captain Scarlet, Lieutenant Green

EQUIPMENT DEPLOYED: Angel Flight, Spectrum Passenger Jet, Spectrum Pursuit Vehicle 503

INCIDENT FILE

INCIDENT ZONE: Frost Line Defence System Network, Canada

INCIDENT REPORT: Frost Line Defence System commander General Ward threatens retaliation against Mysterons following unexplained attacks on hermetically sealed Frost Line bases Red Deer and Cariboo. Captain Scarlet and Lieutenant Green assigned to investigate attacks. Cause found to be sabotage of oxygen supply by Mysteronised maintenance engineer. Scarlet pursues engineer's truck to prevent further attack on Big Bear base. Despite disabling of SPV, Scarlet successfully averts completion of Mysteron agent's mission.

SPECTRAFILE CODE
SHADOW OF FEAR

MYSTERON ACTIVITY

MYSTERON THREAT: 'The eye that dares to look upon our planet has been destroyed. You will never succeed. You will never discover the secret of the Mysterons'

MYSTERON FORCES: Doctor Breck

SPECTRUM RESPONSE

PERSONNEL MOBILISED: Angel Crew (Destiny Angel, Harmony Angel, and one other), Melody Angel, Captain Blue, Captain Grey, Captain Scarlet

EQUIPMENT DEPLOYED: Angel Flight, Spectrum Pursuit Vehicle, Spectrum Helicopter

INCIDENT FILE

INCIDENT ZONE: K14 Observatory, Nepal

INCIDENT REPORT: As part of Operation Sword a mini satellite is soft landed on Martian moon Phobus, following anticipated Mysteron destruction of decoy satellite, to survey planet and transmit photographs to K14 observatory. While reception of transmissions is awaited, astronomer Breck disappears and is suspected to be under Mysteron control. Breck is located following Spectrum search and is shot during gun battle with Blue and Scarlet after revealing that he has planted a bomb in the observatory rotation gear housing. Before warning can be given observatory is rotated to receive mini satellite transmission and explosives are detonated, destroying installation.

SPECTRAFILE CODE
THE HEART OF NEW YORK

MYSTERON ACTIVITY

MYSTERON THREAT: 'We've seen the greed and corruption of the world in which you live and will take our revenge upon it. We will destroy the heart of New York'

MYSTERON FORCES: Captain Black

SPECTRUM RESPONSE

PERSONNEL MOBILISED: Captain Blue, Captain Magenta, Captain Ochre, Captain Scarlet, Spectrum New York Security Unit

EQUIPMENT DEPLOYED: Spectrum Passenger Jet, Spectrum Saloon Cars

INCIDENT FILE

INCIDENT ZONE: New York City

INCIDENT REPORT: Sophisticated break-in at Spectrum Security Vault results in theft by criminal gang of highly confidential files detailing Mysteron activity. Posing as Mysteron agents, gang attempt to rob New York vault of Second National Bank under cover of latest Mysteron threat. Investigations into gang movements by Captains Blue and Scarlet result in positive identification of Captain Black in vicinity of bank. Pursuit of Black ends inconclusively when Mysteron agent dematerialises in dead end street. Gang subsequently perish in explosive detonation of bank, engineered by Black.

SPECTRAFILE CODE
FIRE AT RIG 15

MYSTERON ACTIVITY

MYSTERON THREAT: 'We have observed the pathetic attempts of Spectrum to combat us and we have decided to render them powerless. We intend to immobilise the whole of Spectrum'

MYSTERON FORCES: Captain Black, Jason Smith

SPECTRUM RESPONSE

PERSONNEL MOBILISED: Angel Flight (Melody and two others), Captain Blue, Captain Scarlet

EQUIPMENT DEPLOYED: Angel Flight, Spectrum Passenger Jet, Spectrum Pursuit Vehicle 1034

INCIDENT FILE

INCIDENT ZONE: Bensheba Refinery and Ultrasonic Deep Wells, Arabia

INCIDENT REPORT: Assigned to monitor security at Bensheba oil field, Captains Blue and Scarlet discover attempt by fire-fighter Jason Smith to detroy Bensheba refinery using explosives-laden truck following Mysteronisation during operation to cap oil leak at ultrasonic drilling rig. Captain Scarlet pursues vehicle in SPV, successfully forcing it away from refinery to avert destruction of installation. Despite suffering potentially fatal injuries in explosive collision with oil storage tank after losing control of SPV, Scarlet later makes full recovery.

SPECTRAFILES

SPECTRAFILE CODE
THE LAUNCHING

MYSTERON ACTIVITY

MYSTERON THREAT: 'We will destroy President Roberts within the next 12 hours'

MYSTERON FORCES: Captain Black, Mervin Brand

SPECTRUM RESPONSE

PERSONNEL MOBILISED: Angel Crew (Destiny, Harmony, Symphony), Captain Blue, Captain Ochre, Captain Scarlet, Spectrum Ground Forces

EQUIPMENT DEPLOYED: Angel Flight, Spectrum Saloon Cars

INCIDENT FILE

INCIDENT ZONE: Trans-Pacific Shipping Corporation Shipyard

INCIDENT REPORT: Security cordon set up around North American head of state President Roberts under command of Captain Blue to provide protection against latest Mysteron threat with Angel Flight patrolling restricted air space surrounding area of presidential residence. Journalist Mervin Brand cautioned after intrusion into restricted air space and escorted to nearby airfield by Harmony Angel.

Following realisation by Captain Scarlet that new atomic liner named after president may be Mysteron target, Scarlet drives to dockyard to deliver warning to shipping company vice-president. Attempt by Brand to destroy ship through exertion of Mysteron influence over champagne bottle successfully prevented by Scarlet just prior to launch. Despite sustaining potentially fatal injuries during subsequent explosion, Scarlet later makes full recovery.

SPECTRAFILE CODE
LUNARVILLE 7

MYSTERON ACTIVITY

MYSTERON THREAT: 'We have no quarrel with the Moon, and we accept their offer of friendship, but we will continue to take our revenge against the Earth'

MYSTERON FORCES: Lunar Controller, Orson

SPECTRUM RESPONSE

PERSONNEL MOBILISED: Captain Blue, Captain Scarlet, Lieutenant Green

EQUIPMENT DEPLOYED: No Spectrum Equipment Deployed

INCIDENT FILE

INCIDENT ZONE: Lunarville 7, the Moon

INCIDENT REPORT: Captain Blue, Captain Scarlet and Lieutenant Green sent to Moon to deliver personal message from World President to Lunar Controller following claims he has made direct contact with the Mysterons and that he has declared that the Moon will not support Earth in the current conflict. Prior to arrival agents also requested to investigate reports that new unauthorised complex is being constructed in the Humboldt Sea. Investigations confirm reports of complex construction, revealing it to be Lunar Mysteron City and expose Lunar Controller and aide as Mysteron agents. Following departure of Spectrum agents Lunarville 7 destroyed due to malfunction of computer control system.

SPECTRAFILE CODE
THE TRAP

MYSTERON ACTIVITY

MYSTERON THREAT: 'At the appointed hour, as the clock is chiming, the wings of the world will be clipped'

MYSTERON FORCES: Commander Goddard, Holt

SPECTRUM RESPONSE

PERSONNEL MOBILISED: Melody Angel, Symphony Angel, Captain Blue, Captain Scarlet

EQUIPMENT DEPLOYED: Angel Escort, Angel Search Flight, Spectrum Passenger Jet, Spectrum Saloon Car, Spectrum Pursuit Vehicle A75, World Air Force Command Security Flight Magnacopter

INCIDENT FILE

INCIDENT ZONE: Glen Garry Castle, Scotland

INCIDENT REPORT: Captain Scarlet assigned to carry out security review of World Air Force Supreme Command conference venue before confirming clearance prior to arrival of delegates. On arrival by Magnacopter following hoax clearance report, Symphony Angel discovers security of venue has been compromised and that Command Security officer Goddard and assistant are Mysteron agents before being confined in dungeon with Scarlet. Discovery of wrecked World Air Force Security aircraft XQR by Melody Angel raises alarm and Captain Blue sent to Glen Garry to investigate. Successful escape by Scarlet and Symphony from dungeon enables Scarlet to prevent hypermatic machine gun attack on delegates. Despite sustaining fatal wounds during action to allow evacuation of delegates, Scarlet later makes full recovery.

SPECTRAFILE CODE
MODEL SPY

MYSTERON ACTIVITY

MYSTERON THREAT: 'We are about to attack the House of Verdain. Andre Verdain will die'

MYSTERON FORCES: Captain Black, Gabrielle, Helga

SPECTRUM RESPONSE

PERSONNEL MOBILISED: Destiny Angel, Symphony Angel, Captain Blue, Captain Scarlet

EQUIPMENT DEPLOYED: Spectrum Pursuit Vehicle (unclassified), Requisitioned Helicopter

INCIDENT FILE

INCIDENT ZONE: Principality of Monte Carlo

INCIDENT REPORT: Working undercover, Captain Blue, Captain Scarlet, and Destiny and Symphony Angels are assigned to protect Andre Verdain in Monte Carlo. Following suspected but unconfirmed Mysteron sabotage of pleasure yacht, Captain Black later seen making attempt to kill Verdain during party. Blackout caused by Mysteron agent Gabrielle allows Black to escape with Verdain and Mysteron agent Helga. Tracer drug slipped into drink given to Verdain facilitates Spectrum pursuit by air and road. Mysteron agents abandon Verdain in road tunnel blocked by local police and subsequently dematerialise.

SPECTRAFILE CODE
TRAITOR

MYSTERON ACTIVITY

MYSTERON THREAT: 'The Spectrum organisation will be torn apart from within. The traitor among you will create havoc and destroy morale'

MYSTERON FORCES: Mechanical Component

SPECTRUM RESPONSE

PERSONNEL MOBILISED: Angel Crew (Destiny, Harmony, Melody), Captain Blue, Captain Scarlet

EQUIPMENT DEPLOYED: Angel Flight, Spectrum Passenger Jet, Spectrum Hovercraft

INCIDENT FILE

INCIDENT ZONE: Base Koala, Australia

INCIDENT REPORT: Captain Blue and Captain Scarlet assigned to carry out undercover investigations at Base Koala following series of suspected hovercraft sabotage incidents to ascertain possible connection with Mysteron threat. On recommencement of hovercraft operations Blue and Scarlet accompany cadets on patrol in Hovercraft 4. During recurrence of mechanical malfunction, Scarlet orders Blue and cadets to abandon vehicle while remaining on board to attempt removal of instruments recorder. Actions result in his sustaining potentially fatal injuries as a result of explosive detonation of hovercraft, from which he later makes full recovery. Salvaged recorder reveals cause of mechanical failure to be Mysteronised valve component.

SPECTRAFILE CODE
SPECIAL ASSIGNMENT

MYSTERON ACTIVITY

MYSTERON THREAT: 'We will deal another crushing blow. We told you we intend to obliterate the sub-continent of North America'

MYSTERON FORCES: Captain Black, Mason's Autos Attendant, Kramer, Steele

SPECTRUM RESPONSE

PERSONNEL MOBILISED: Angel Crew (Harmony, Melody, Rhapsody), Captain Blue, Captain Scarlet

EQUIPMENT DEPLOYED: Angel Flight, Spectrum Pursuit Vehicle 104

INCIDENT FILE

INCIDENT ZONE: Arizona, North America

INCIDENT REPORT: Acting on report received by Spectrum Intelligence, Captain Scarlet assigned to pose undercover as gambling addict to engineer dismissal from Spectrum and present himself as target for Mysteron agents operating in Arizona. Acting on own initiative, Captain Blue follows Scarlet to meeting and is shot by Scarlet with tranquiliser gun after learning that Mysteron target is Nuclear City. Under instructions from Mysterons armed with atomic trigger Scarlet requisitions SPV to launch attack on Nuclear City but is intercepted by Spectrum Angels alerted by Captain Blue. Scarlet receives potentially fatal injuries before ejecting from SPV prior to its destruction, but effects full recovery.

SPECTRAFILES

SPECTRAFILE CODE
CRATER 101

MYSTERON ACTIVITY

MYSTERON THREAT: 'Although you may have discovered our complex on the Moon, it will never reveal its secrets. Anyone who dares to enter will be destroyed. You have been warned'

MYSTERON FORCES: Lunar Technician Fraser

SPECTRUM RESPONSE

PERSONNEL MOBILISED: Captain Blue, Captain Scarlet, Lieutenant Green

EQUIPMENT DEPLOYED: No Spectrum Equipment Deployed

INCIDENT FILE

INCIDENT ZONE: Crater 101, the Moon

INCIDENT REPORT: Volunteer team formed by Captain Blue, Captain Scarlet and Lieutenant Green to carry out mission to remove power source from Mysteron Lunar Complex prior to destruction of complex by lunar authorities with low yield atomic device. Travelling from Lunarville 6 by Moonmobile, Spectrum team transfer to Moon Tractor to engage and destroy Mysteron defence vehicles and gain entry to complex. During transportation of atomic device to area by Lunar Tank, Lunar technician Fraser discovered to be Mysteron agent and that device detonation timing has been altered to take place ahead of schedule. Lunarville 6 controller launches unmanned rocket to warn Spectrum team. Captain Scarlet successfully removes pulsator power source from complex and escapes moments before atomic detonation.

SPECTRAFILE CODE
NOOSE OF ICE

MYSTERON ACTIVITY

MYSTERON THREAT: 'Your much boasted new space fleet is doomed to failure. We will make certain you never return to our planet Mars'

MYSTERON FORCES: Captain Black, Technician Nielson

SPECTRUM RESPONSE

PERSONNEL MOBILISED: Captain Blue, Captain Scarlet

EQUIPMENT DEPLOYED: Spectrum Pursuit Vehicle

INCIDENT FILE

INCIDENT ZONE: Hot Spot Mining Complex, North Pole

INCIDENT REPORT: Captain Blue and Captain Scarlet assigned to investigate special areas of importance to space fleet programme at Space Administration HQ and identify Hot Spot Tritonium mining complex as potential Mysteron target. During inspection visit at site, technician Nielson discovered to be Mysteron agent. When power to Hot Spot tower Alpha Circuit cut from Eskimo Booster Station trapping Spectrum agents and mine personnel below surface, Captain Scarlet returns to surface through use of diving suit and confronts Mysteron agent in booster station. Despite sustaining potentially fatal injuries Scarlet eliminates Mysteron agent by means of electrocution and restores power to complex. Scarlet subsequently makes full recovery from injuries.

SPECTRAFILE CODE
DANGEROUS RENDEZVOUS

MYSTERON ACTIVITY

MYSTERON THREAT: 'Our next act of retaliation will be to destroy Cloudbase. Do you hear? Spectrum's headquarters Cloudbase will be destroyed at midnight'

MYSTERON FORCES: Captain Black, Mysteron Pulsator

SPECTRUM RESPONSE

PERSONNEL MOBILISED: Angel Escort (Destiny), Captain Scarlet, Captain Ochre

EQUIPMENT DEPLOYED: Angel Aircraft, Spectrum Saloon Car, Spectrum Helicopter, Yellow Fox VIP Transporter, Spectrum Passenger Jet

INCIDENT FILE

INCIDENT ZONE: Greenland

INCIDENT REPORT: Captain Scarlet assigned to escort Doctor Kurnitz from the Nash Institute of Technology to Cloudbase to install Mysteron Pulsator in simulator to enable transmission of message to Mysterons. Acting on instructions issued in Mysteron response, Captain Scarlet flies unarmed and without communication devices to Greenland for meeting with Mysteron representative. On arrival at pre-arranged meeting after abandoning aircraft by ejecting, Scarlet discovers meeting is a trap, but escapes having witnessed destructive power of small pulsator. From nearby communication relay station Scarlet successfully transmits Morse code warning to Cloudbase that pulsator is booby trap. Acting on warning, Captain Ochre jettisons pulsator from simulator room allowing it to explode harmlessly within seconds ahead of deadline expiration.

SPECTRAFILE CODE
FLIGHT 104

MYSTERON ACTIVITY

MYSTERON THREAT: 'The conference at Lake Toma will be sabotaged. We know what you are trying to do, but you will not succeed'

MYSTERON FORCES: Captain Black, Flight 104

SPECTRUM RESPONSE

PERSONNEL MOBILISED: Angel Crew (Destiny, Harmony, Rhapsody), Captain Blue, Captain Grey, Captain Magenta, Captain Ochre, Captain Scarlet

EQUIPMENT DEPLOYED: Angel Flight

INCIDENT FILE

INCIDENT ZONE: European Airspace

INCIDENT REPORT: Undercover operation by Captain Blue and Captain Scarlet to escort Doctor Conrad to Martian Mission Evaluation Conference arouses suspicion of two journalists. Journalists allowed to join pre-block booked commercial flight to Geneva as security precaution, but during flight aircraft discovered to be under Mysteron control. Attempts to re-establish control of aircraft succeed due to influence of electrical generation ground station. Damage to undercarriage control circuits sustained as a result of action taken to gain entry to flight deck leads Scarlet to carry out forced landing of aircraft at Geneva airport. During landing Scarlet suffers potentially fatal injuries but successfully effects full recovery.

SPECTRAFILE CODE
PLACE OF THE ANGELS

MYSTERON ACTIVITY

MYSTERON THREAT: 'To prove how useless it is for you to resist us we will destroy the place of the angels'

MYSTERON FORCES: Captain Black, Judith Chapman

SPECTRUM RESPONSE

PERSONNEL MOBILISED: Angel Crew (Destiny, Harmony, Symphony), Captain Blue, Captain Scarlet, All Spectrum Agencies on worldwide alert

EQUIPMENT DEPLOYED: Angel Flight, Spectrum Passenger Jet, Spectrum Pursuit Vehicle 021

INCIDENT FILE

INCIDENT ZONE: Manchester England, New York, Los Angeles

INCIDENT REPORT: Captains Blue and Scarlet assigned to investigate theft of phial containing K14 virus from Biological Research Station D by Mysteronised research assistant Judith Chapman. All Spectrum agencies put on worldwide red alert to locate Chapman. Sighting in New York results in pursuit of Chapman by Blue and Scarlet in SPV but Mysteron agent evades capture by staging hoax virus spillage. Following precautionary decontamination procedure, Blue and Scarlet reassigned to continue search. Report of further sighting in Los Angeles area proves positive with potential Mysteron target identified as Boulder Dam. Parachuting on to parapet of dam Scarlet confronts Chapman, causing her to drop phial and fall from structure. Despite gunshot wounds sustained during confrontation, Scarlet retrieves phial and subsequently makes full recovery.

SPECTRAFILE CODE
CODE NAME EUROPA

MYSTERON ACTIVITY

MYSTERON THREAT: 'We will destroy the Triumvirate of Europe. The Triumvirate of Europe will be destroyed'

MYSTERON FORCES: Captain Black, Professor Gabriel Carney

SPECTRUM RESPONSE

PERSONNEL MOBILISED: Angel Crew (Destiny and two others), Captain Blue, Captain Ochre, Captain Magenta, Captain Scarlet, Spectrum Guards, Spectrum Ground Forces

EQUIPMENT DEPLOYED: Angel Flight, Spectrum Passenger Jet, Spectrum Pursuit Vehicle (unclassified), Spectrum Saloon Cars

INCIDENT FILE

INCIDENT ZONE: Continent of Europe

INCIDENT REPORT: After Mysteron attempt to kill Triumvirate of Europe member Conrad Olafson at Vandom Maximum Security Base fails following implementation of security plan XB, Professor Gabriel Carney discovered to be Mysteron agent. Search of Carney's residence reveals that John L. Henderson is next intended target. Carney's car reported in area of Maximum Security Centre, but attempts at pursuit by Captains Blue and Scarlet in SPV ineffective due to activation by Carney of electronic jamming device. Mysteron agent's attempt to kill Henderson at Maximum Security Centre following sabotage of building's communication system and power supply successfully thwarted by Scarlet through deployment of high tensile booby trap.

SPECTRAFILE CODE
TREBLE CROSS

MYSTERON ACTIVITY

MYSTERON THREAT: 'We intend to deal another devastating blow. We will destroy the world capital Futura City. Futura will be razed to the ground'

MYSTERON FORCES: Captain Black, Major Gravener

SPECTRUM RESPONSE

PERSONNEL MOBILISED: Angel Crew (Destiny, Harmony, Rhapsody), Captain Blue, Captain Ochre, Captain Scarlet, Spectrum Road Block Operatives

EQUIPMENT DEPLOYED: Angel Flight, Spectrum Pursuit Vehicle (unclassified), Spectrum Detector Trucks

INCIDENT FILE

INCIDENT ZONE: Slaton World Air Force Base and Western Airbase, Canada

INCIDENT REPORT: Acting on information received from Slaton World Air Force Base, Captain Blue and Captain Scarlet investigate report of attempted theft of armed XK107 atomic bomber by doppelganger of chief test pilot Major Gravener. Double believed to be Mysteron duplicate of Gravener created following his near death in car accident, fatal consequences of which having been prevented by his rescue and resuscitation by passing Slaton hospital specialists. Revived Gravener volunteers to assist Spectrum in attempt to reveal Mysterons' plan of attack on Futura City. Identification of rendezvous point as airstrip located at Western Airbase leads to sealing of facility by Spectrum forces, but potential hope of apprehending Captain Black unrealised when suspect contact proves to be Mysteron reconstruction of World Air Force Base driver Harris.

SPECTRAFILE CODE
INFERNO

MYSTERON ACTIVITY

MYSTERON THREAT: 'Our next act of retaliation will be to destroy the complex at Nahama. Nahama will be destroyed'

MYSTERON FORCES: Captain Black, SKR Rocket Capsule

SPECTRUM RESPONSE

PERSONNEL MOBILISED: Angel Crew (Destiny, Rhapsody, Symphony), Captain Blue, Captain Magenta, Captain Ochre, Captain Scarlet

EQUIPMENT DEPLOYED: Angel Flight, Spectrum Pursuit Vehicle (unclassified)

INCIDENT FILE

INCIDENT ZONE: Nahama Complex, Andes Mountains

INCIDENT REPORT: Captains Blue, Magenta, Ochre and Scarlet assigned to monitor Nahama Complex to prevent possible attacks. Report received from Eurospace Tracker Station indicates potential threat posed by SKR4 space recovery vehicle equipped with high explosives and believed to be under Mysteron control. Capsule discovered to be on crash course with Nahama area under guidance of homing beacon sited in ancient temple overlooking complex. As insufficient time available to locate and shut down device, Angel Flight ordered to mount air strike against structure to destroy beacon. Beacon remains operative despite destruction of temple leading capsule to crashland on site. Impact results in landslide destroying large parts of Nahama complex.

SPECTRAFILE CODE
EXPO 2068

MYSTERON ACTIVITY

MYSTERON THREAT: 'Disaster will strike the Atlantic seaboard of North America. We will deal a heavy blow to the prestige of the world'

MYSTERON FORCES: Captain Black, Atomic Reactor Transporter 43

SPECTRUM RESPONSE

PERSONNEL MOBILISED: Angel Crew (Destiny and two others), Captain Blue, Captain Scarlet

EQUIPMENT DEPLOYED: Angel Flight, Spectrum Pursuit Vehicle 442, Jet Pack, Spectrum Helicopter

INCIDENT FILE

INCIDENT ZONE: Expo 2068 site and surrounding area, Canada

INCIDENT REPORT: Assigned to monitor transportation of compact core reactor to Manicougan dam site by road, Captain Blue and Captain Scarlet alerted of transporter's failure to pass through designated checkpoint. Investigations lead Blue and Scarlet to discover wounded forestry worker and discarded thermal valve in clearing. Witness statement by wounded worker links reactor disappearance to helicopters operated by Seneca company at nearby expo site. Suspect helicopter tracked to site where Scarlet gains access to cargo crate containing reactor with aid of jet pack and successfully shuts down device, averting nuclear detonation. Following destruction of helicopter and cargo crate, Scarlet suffers potentially fatal wounds, but later makes full recovery.

SPECTRAFILE CODE
FLIGHT TO ATLANTICA

MYSTERON ACTIVITY

MYSTERON THREAT: 'We intend to destroy the World Navy complex at Atlantica. Atlantica will be annihilated'

MYSTERON FORCES: Captain Black, Non-alcoholic Champagne

SPECTRUM RESPONSE

PERSONNEL MOBILISED: Angel Crew (Symphony, Destiny, Melody), Colonel White, Captain Blue, Captain Ochre, Captain Scarlet

EQUIPMENT DEPLOYED: Angel Flight, Spectrum Passenger Jet

INCIDENT FILE

INCIDENT ZONE: Atlantica Base, Atlantic Ocean

INCIDENT REPORT: On reception of Mysteron threat, Angel Flight launched to patrol Atlantica Base airspace, and Captains Blue and Ochre assigned as replacement mission pilots to carry out scheduled aerial bombing of dangerous wreck sites in vicinity of base. When Angel Flight and other base personnel found to be acting in irresponsible and undisciplined manner, Colonel White and Captain Scarlet discover champagne served at unsanctioned social to be contaminated with disinhibiting organic compound. Realising potential danger to Atlantica from similarly intoxicated bomber crew White and Scarlet attempt to intercept bomber in SPJ. When crew fail to respond to warnings, Scarlet ordered to destroy rogue aircraft and accedes only moments after crew safely eject. Despite destruction of outer defences, Atlantica Base otherwise unaffected by attack.

SPECTRAFILE CODE
ATTACK ON CLOUDBASE

(File Under: Symphony Angel, Heat Stroke Induced Hallucination)

MYSTERON ACTIVITY

MYSTERON THREAT: (Imagined) 'Spectrum's headquarters Cloudbase is our next objective. We will spare no effort to ensure that Cloudbase is totally destroyed'

MYSTERON FORCES: (Imagined) Captain Black, Mysteron Invasion Fleet

SPECTRUM RESPONSE

PERSONNEL MOBILISED: Symphony Angel, Destiny Angel, Captain Blue, Captain Scarlet, Spectrum Search and Rescue Team

EQUIPMENT DEPLOYED: Angel Aircraft, Spectrum Search and Rescue Vehicles

INCIDENT FILE

INCIDENT ZONE: Sahara Desert

INCIDENT REPORT: On return from routine patrol, Symphony Angel reports suspected air strike and ejects from crashlanding aircraft. Search and rescue operation mounted and Symphony eventually located. During subsequent medical examination by Doctor Fawn, Symphony recounts hallucinatory dream of attack on Cloudbase and subsequent destruction by Mysteron flying saucer fleet. Following thorough health check, Symphony passed as fit to resume duty.

SPECTRAFILE CODE
THE INQUISITION

MYSTERON ACTIVITY

MYSTERON THREAT: 'We have observed the Spectrum organisation's attempts to counter us, but one of the members of Spectrum will betray you all'

MYSTERON FORCES: Colgan

SPECTRUM RESPONSE

PERSONNEL MOBILISED: Captain Scarlet, Spectrum Search Team

EQUIPMENT DEPLOYED: Spectrum Pursuit Vehicle (unclassified)

INCIDENT FILE

INCIDENT ZONE: Thames Valley, England

INCIDENT REPORT: Following regular off-duty visit with Captain Scarlet to Markham Arms restaurant near town of Maidenhead, Captain Blue drugged and abducted. Investigations instigated by Captain Scarlet lead to abandoned Thames Valley film studio, where Blue discovered to have been held captive in replica of Cloudbase control room by Mysteron agent Colgan posing as Spectrum Intelligence Agency officer. Mysteron agent reported to have made unsuccessful attempt to deceive Blue into revealing Spectrum cipher codes. Arriving at scene in SPV, Scarlet discovers Blue to have effected escape, and destroys studio building.